SHADOWLAND

A Novel

By

WF Waldrip

WF Waldrip

Shadowland

WF Waldrip is an attorney, adventurer, and novelist. Since childhood Waldrip dreamed of writing stories that readers would enjoy. He is the author of *The Man With Two Last Names*, *The Guards Themselves*, *Honor Among Thieves* and *The Float.*

BOOKS BY WF WALDRIP

Shadowland

The Man with Two Last Names

The Float

Honor Among Thieves

The Guards Themselves

Shadowland

WF Waldrip

FIRST PHARAOH Paperback EDITION

MAY 2020

Maps and illustrations by M. Azurdia

For all parents who read to their children. Or should.

Death is a veil which those who live call life: they
sleep, and it is lifted.

Shelly

Prometheus Unbound

But now, inasmuch as the soul is manifestly immortal,
there is no release or salvation from evil except the
attainment of the highest virtue and wisdom. For the
soul, when on her progress to the world below, takes
nothing with her but nurture and education; and
these are said greatly to benefit or greatly to injure the
departed, at the very beginning of his journey thither.

Plato

Phaedo

As above, so below.

The Emerald Tablet

I

"Nonsense. All these self-styled 'mystics' and 'psychics' are charlatans in my book. I never cease to be amazed at the credulity of people who embrace such hokum," remarked Freeman, loftily.

"I absolutely agree that such subjects have traditionally smacked of fraud, but you certainly can't throw the baby out with the bathwater. Look at acupuncture. It works although science, insofar as I know, hasn't the slightest idea why. How do you explain that?" Parsons was merely playing the devil's advocate, knowing full well that his chess partner disliked having his opinions challenged.

"The mind, the mind," replied Freeman, absently, as he captured Parson's other knight. "If you think something works, then it does...or at least you've convinced yourself that it does. That's all there is to it. Like religious ecstasy, for example; people glimpse heaven as they hear God talking. Or so they want to believe. No rational person would even attempt to dissuade them from their delusions. For such simpletons it is an objective, absolute fact."

"Maybe, maybe not. Maybe at certain times people *do* become more sensitive to higher levels of consciousness. Maybe the gods really *do* appear to them during these periods and it's we who simply refuse to acknowledge it."

The older man leaned his weathered frame back in his chair and sucked on his pipe several times before responding. Exhaling in that luxuriant manner acquired only through many years of pipe smoking, he fixed his gaze on Parsons.

"I've traversed the length and breadth of the globe, seen things that would probably make you age twenty years where you sit, and done things that would most assuredly have gotten me hanged in any even halfway civilized culture. In all my life, however, I've never been presented a shred of evidence that would cause me to alter my disdain for the entire field of the 'psychic,' the 'occult,' or whatever you wish to call it, and its gullible devotees." Freeman loved to talk about his life, and spoke as though his pronouncements on any subject should prove adequate to foreclose further discussion.

The younger man, having just captured one of Freeman's pawns, started to reply when his attention was diverted by the sight of another habitué of the Olympus Club. Chatting with another member was a tall, thin man only four or five years his senior. Although standing with his back toward the two men at the chessboard, Parsons immediately recognized him by his slightly slumping posture and wavy brown hair.

"Art, hello!"

Turning, Arthur Alexander Smith begged a hasty good day of his companion and sauntered over to the game board. Having been a member of the Olympus Club since his retirement from military service two years earlier, Smith kept largely to himself. Although some Olympians secretly resented Smith's detachment and, indeed, questioned why he even bothered to maintain his membership, he shrugged that his retirement income entitled him to indulge a few whims, of which membership in the exclusive Olympus Club was one, and that, "being divorced with no children, I'm allowed the luxury of squandering my money on whatever I wish."

Smith rarely spoke of his life as a professional soldier. Having enlisted at an early age, however, he was able to enjoy the fruits of retirement earlier than most of the club's other members. Unlike most of them, who were socially distinguished or prominent in the professional community, he had no apparent interest in business and confessed total indifference to world affairs. These peculiarities notwithstanding, he was amiable and popular with those Olympians whom he chose to befriend.

"Hello, Paul, Leonard. Who's winning?" he asked, casually scanning the board.

"Leonard is, if you consider sacrificing a rook and both bishops, not to mention half of his pawns, winning," grinned Parsons. "Long time no see. What brings the Prodigal Son back to the fold?"

"I'm going on vacation tomorrow and figured I'd stop in before leaving. Besides, I've been hearing rumors that I'm dead and thought it best to set the record straight."

"I envy you, Art. My vacations consist of playing chess and disabusing Parsons of his innumerable follies," Freeman gravely intoned.

"Sounds serious," said Smith with mock solemnity. "I trust I'm not intruding. I assumed you already knew about the birds and the bees, Paul."

Parsons snorted. "I'll never understand the birds and the bees, but that's not what we've been discussing. I innocently mentioned to Leonard that Drachovich is in town, and that led to his launching into a harangue about the evils of..."

"Gullibility," finished Freeman.

"Who's Drachovich?"

"A Russian mystical philosopher. He recently established a colony in France to promulgate his teachings and is now touring America, trying to drum up converts."

"And money," added Freeman.

"He sounds like a wannabe Jim Jones," Smith grinned. "What's the matter, Leonard, do you have something against Russians?"

"No, but I *do* have something against foolish sensationalism."

Parsons explained, "Leonard is convinced that there's no such thing as a genuine mystical experience. I am somewhat more reticent to condemn the entire subject. Who are we to say what is, or isn't, real? Take Freeman's queen, for example," he lifted the chess piece from the board and began gesturing with it as Freeman scowled. "Were I to ask you the color of this queen, you would undoubtedly answer 'black.' While correct, how do I know that what *you* see as the color black is the same as what I see as black? In other words, Freeman's queen might actually be red to you, but to you red is 'black,' while to me it's red." He replaced the queen back on the board and Freeman reached across to adjust it to her former position. "Am I making any sense? My point is, it's impossible to establish the nature of reality with absolute certainty because *your* perception of what's real may not be the same as mine...what's 'real' to you may not be 'real' to me."

Turning to Freeman, Smith remarked, "I remember that when I was a little kid, both of my maternal grandparents were avowed spiritualists. They used to hold séances, and claimed to be in direct communication with those in the 'next sphere', as they referred to it. For years after my great grandmother died, they claimed that she sent them regular messages from the grave...she and a whole cast of others, as well. I didn't know what to make of it then and still don't."

"If you ask me, it's like I explained to our impressionable friend here," pontificated Freeman. "If you believe something badly enough, then for all intents and purposes it's real. Any sensible person would dismiss it as complete rubbish but, subjectively speaking, it's as real as this table. I daresay that your grandparents were probably communicating with their own psyches rather than with any independent intelligences...like Dickens said, 'more gravy than grave,' or some such."

"There's something to be said for that," agreed Smith. "Only I have a difficult time handling such profundities when I'm thirsty. You two philosophers want anything?" As Smith ambled off toward the bar his companions redirected their attention to their half-forgotten chess match.

II

Smith's bedside clock showed exactly thirty-six minutes past midnight. Arriving home from the Olympus Club at 11:30, he had promptly retired in order to be fresh for his morning flight. Abruptly awake now, he squinted about in astonishment.

His bedroom was ablaze with light. Emanating from no discernable source, a lustrous whiteness permeated the very air, starkly exposing the room's smallest details. Every corner and angle were awash with radiant intensity. The bedroom furniture, the normally hidden recesses, even the slight irregularities in the painted walls were brilliantly illuminated. It was as though a multitude of arc lights were focused directly on the interior of Smith's bedroom.

Smith attempted to shield his eyes against the glare with one hand as he tossed back the coverlet and swung his legs to the floor. Although he had shaken off the cobwebs of sleep, he was utterly baffled by luminosity of his bedroom.

"What...?" he muttered, overwhelmed.

Smith stood and stepped across the room to the window. Parting the curtains, he fully expected to be assailed by the blinding headlights from a neighbor's automobile. Nothing. The night was unpierced by all but the icy light of the stars. He turned away from the window, bewildered.

Smith exited the bedroom and strode rapidly through the other rooms of the house. Everything appeared to be in order, the interior of his home silent and dark. Only Smith's bedroom was ablaze with inexplicable light, and to it he returned.

The searing illumination had not abated and, indeed, seemed to have increased in magnitude. It permeated every square inch of the room and its vibrant intensity rendered the creation of any shadow impossible.

Except for one.

Near the head of Smith's bed reared a stark shadow. He had initially failed to give it any notice because his entire attention had been consumed by the baffling radiance that filled the room. Now, as he squinted about, he perceived the shadow.

Though cast by no identifiable object, the shadow was sharply defined against the wall and occupied an area about two feet wide from floor to ceiling. Though perplexed by the bewildering luminosity of his bedroom, Smith was equally intrigued by the curious shadow that now captured his attention. He gingerly approached it for closer examination and extended an exploratory hand.

Something from within the shadow grabbed his outstretched arm.

Astonished, Smith jerked awkwardly backward but was unable to free himself. In less time than it takes to describe, he was pulled roughly into the ebony portal.

"Ouch!" He was yanked unceremoniously over a two-foot precipice and landed squarely on his bare knees. "What is this? I've had some strange dreams in my life, but this takes the cake!"

Smith's new environ was an expansive and badly lit room. He clambered to his feet and peered about.

Rudely appointed, the room contained only a few large, rough wooden tables as furnishings, these heavily weighted down with a hodge-podge of archaic scientific paraphernalia: pelicans, flasks, matrasses, and various alembics. A handful of candles crudely melted in their own puddles of wax guttered feebly in the dimness, their smoky flames reflected in the dusty glass of the antiquated equipment. The apparent laboratory was in a state of extreme squalor and appeared to be of considerable age. Insofar as he could ascertain in the murk, the enclosing walls were composed of living rock, blotched here and there with great black patches of lichens. In a word, Smith appeared to be in a cavern, though one totally devoid of any doorway or aperture to account for his presence there.

In the shadows, twenty feet away, stood an anthropomorphic figure.

In the shadows, twenty feet away, stood an anthropomorphic figure.

Really little more than a bundle of rags, the form had unaccountably eluded his gaze during Smith's initial survey of his surroundings. He squinted in disbelief at the specter but, because of the poor lighting, was unable to discern any physical details in the frocked and hooded being.

The figure drifted over and removed from its niche in the wall one of the oil lamps that provided scant illumination to the room. Holding it in front of his body, he gestured toward a heap of rags on one of the tables.

"Dress yourself," he commanded in an imperious voice.

For the first time Smith realized that he was nude. He gingerly approached the table and slowly began to don the musty clothes.

"Who are you and where am I?" Smith confronted his enigmatic host after dressing. He was now convinced that he was indeed awake, but sure of little else.

Instead of addressing himself to the query, the recondite figure turned and began shuffling into the darkest extremes of the capacious room. "The effort required to bring you here has fagged me," spoke he indifferently. "I must now rest." Then he was gone.

Smith strode after the strange being, but his eyes encountered only darkness and his outstretched hands only empty air. Furious, he penetrated deeper into the enveloping darkness, his bare feet padding along the cold stone floor. Nothing. Only massive silence and gloom, the dimly lit laboratory now merely a feeble yellow glow far behind. Apprehensive and angry in equal measure, Smith reluctantly retraced his steps to the seemingly illimitable cavern.

The crumbling equipment in the chamber where Smith found himself exhibited designs long obsolete, relics of laboratories antedating the 17th century. Several of the ancient retorts were filled with inky liquids and connected with an elaborate network of pipes and hoses. Here and there were bottles of green, yellow, and black powders, while a scattering of white granules was carelessly strewn the length of several tables. Heaps of charred wood and coal occupied much of the floor. The room was imbued with an air of great antiquity, of long and fruitless labor.

Smith was frustrated and perplexed. Kicking debris from a spot along one wall, he sat down to puzzle over the affair. Even after a period of intense contemplation no plausible explanation suggested itself to him. He was apparently the victim of some elaborate charade, implemented in an unknown manner by unknown persons for an unknown purpose. Over and over in his mind he turned these questions until, unable to divine meaning in them, he finally dozed off.

When he awoke, he saw what appeared to be the same cloaked personage standing near him. It was impossible to judge the length of Smith's repose; the candles and oil lamps still flickered silently in the semi-darkness. Nothing around him had changed. Although as far as he knew his sleep could have lasted for hours, he felt as though he had slept but a few minutes.

"Who are you?" he demanded, starting up.

"My name is Lasceaux and I am the greatest natural philosopher in this world," came the reply from behind the hood.

"What are you talking about, a 'natural philosopher'? That sounds like pure hogwash!" Smith snarled.

"Fool! As is universally acknowledged by all but stupid geese like you, the ultimate goal of natural philosophers is to obtain spiritual perfection through the transmutation of the dross aspects of our nature into spiritual gold."

Smith glanced at the decaying scientific apparatus that littered the bleak cavern. "Transmute 'dross into gold?' Cut the baloney. It looks to me like you're a wannabe alchemist."

"Because uninitiated simpletons like you are incapable of thinking in more sublime terms, you are forced to invoke prosaic terms such as 'alkimye' in a vain attempt to describe natural philosophy," Lasceaux spat. "I care nothing for the wealth that is an unfortunate corollary to the spiritual perfection I seek. Material gain is utterly abhorrent to me."

"Sure, it is," Smith dryly responded. "So, what do your pretensions have to do with me?" He edged closer to the figure.

The alchemist retreated three steps.

"I brought you here for my own purposes."

"Where is 'here'?" Despite Smith's surreptitious effort to close the distance between them, the figure remained tantalizingly out of reach.

"'Here' is obviously my laboratory. My unparalleled skill as a natural philosopher enabled you to 'walk through the valley of the shadow of death', as promised by your King David. You have cleaved that redoubtable shadow. Welcome to the fabled valley of death: 'paradise'."

"What are you talking about?"

"I brought you from your earthbound station into the sphere which necessarily follows upon it. I leave it to you to surmise my meaning."

Smith didn't know what to make of the bizarre personage before him. After a moment he guardedly asked, "And you claim that you brought me here?"

"I alone possess that ability."

"How? "

"By my skill, which is unequaled," he smugly vaunted.

"*Why* did you bring me here?"

"Because I require that which you can provide."

Smith pondered a moment. "Am I alive?" he finally asked, intending to indulge the figure identifying itself as 'Lasceaux' until he could determine a course of action.

"'Life' is a relative condition," arrogantly responded the self-proclaimed natural philosopher. "Compared to me you are all but dead."

"What, specifically, do you want with me?"

"I have long been searching for the transcendent cynosure to that most exalted of creations: the elixir of life, the universal panacea, heavenly manna, the celestial balm. Said by all to be the substance whereby base metals may be instantly converted into gold...that which is called the Stone of the Philosopher's," harangued the hooded figure. "Even before I entered this world, I had labored fifty-seven of your terrestrial years in an effort to produce it. Many times I came very close, but always I failed perfection, else I would not be here," he said, scornfully. "Here I have been toiling ceaselessly to this same end, but lately determined that I do not possess some of the essential materials to effect its final creation. You will supply me with these."

Smith ignored these ravings. "How did *you* come to this world?" he asked.

"Exhausted from my unceasing labors, I accidently fell into a fire in my laboratory in Toulouse. When I awoke, I found myself here." Smith thought he saw the alchemist lightly shrug as he spoke.

The cowled form, whom Smith had already concluded was insane, was about to speak further when Smith spontaneously leapt at him. The effort caused an instant wave of crippling nausea to sweep over him and Smith stumbled to the stony floor.

"I have prepared some eatables for you," continued his captor, unruffled. "You must replenish your bodily stores before you will be of use to me." He pointed downward, were Smith saw what appeared to be large globes of fruit in a bowl at the alchemist's feet. Although ravenous, he viewed the offering with disdain.

"What is this really all about?" he growled as he struggled to his feet. "I don't know where I am or who you really are, but I've had enough of this game!"

"You brainless wretch." Lasceaux's voice dripped with contempt. "I am the greatest natural philosopher who ever existed, not a trickster! You delude yourself that I arranged an artful deception simply for your amusement, but it is *you* who is truly the fool. You are here to serve at my pleasure!" He withdrew from the folds of his wormy garment a small container. Opening it, he swiftly cast a portion of its contents on his wobbly captive. Feeling at first like droplets of water, the substance quickly began to emit intense heat, burning hatefully into Smith's flesh like white phosphorous. Frantically he attempted to brush it off, but the faster he brushed the more agonizing became the heat.

"Welcome my own special variety of Greek fire," cackled Lasceaux. "Cause me no trouble and you will be spared its wrath. Now eat!" He roughly kicked the bowl of fruit toward his prisoner.

The alchemist removed a fluttering oil lamp from a niche in the lichened wall and seated himself at a table, where he opened massive tome and began to read in the marginal light. Defeated for the present, Smith squatted on the stony floor and removed from the basket one of the edibles, the mealy pulp of which he reluctantly began to chew.

III

He must have slept again; he couldn't remember for certain. Placed near his head was a shallow earthen dish of fetid water. Parched, he quaffed it though its bitterness made him gag. Smith was cold and hungry and sore. And frightened. He looked up to see the shadowy Lasceaux drift in soundlessly, carrying a laden tray.

"Here are victuals. I believe that you will find them somewhat more palatable than simple fruit," spoke the faceless alchemist without compassion as he set the platter down on an area of table unburdened with scientific paraphernalia. He stepped away from the table and gestured toward the food.

Smith rose shakily to his feet, stood weaving as a bolt of pain shot through his head, and stepped dubiously toward the uncertain viands. As he did, the wholesome aroma of roasted meat greeted his nostrils. He quickened his step to the plate of food, saliva flooding his mouth. What he saw on the dish made him wretch.

Heaped on the platter was a pile of crudely dismembered parts of human bodies: children, judging from the size of the pieces. Smith could identify small arms with hands still attached, perfectly formed legs, and sections of torso split open through the sternum.

"Oh, God," he moaned.

"Eat," commanded Lasceaux. "You must replenish yourself."

"I will not!" cried Smith, his voice echoing throughout the stone chamber. Without waiting for a response, he sprang at the malevolent alchemist, intending to throttle his vile neck. Unperturbed, his captor merely tossed a quantity of the incendiary powder upon him. Smith fell helplessly upon the floor as the substance sizzled into his flesh.

Lasceaux walked to his defenseless victim, directed repeated kicks into his prostrate body, and showered him with violent curses in French. His rage spent, the alchemist turned back to the table, where he seated himself on a rickety stool indifferently hewn from wood. Cataleptic, Smith watched from the rocky floor as the alchemist began to devour the meat with manifest relish.

Lasceaux wiped his mouth on his cassock as he ate. "Suit yourself, as your value to me resides only in your corporeal components, which are necessary to my work. My endeavors toward creating the Philosopher's Stone, Monsieur Smith, have unfortunately been hampered because of the paucity of certain necessary essences...galena, zinc, antimony, iron, and others," he disclosed. "These substances do not occur naturally in this locality; I previously obtained sufficient quantities of them from a Kaelopian trader, in whose land they occur naturally in great abundance. I recently received information, however, that my supplier's vessel fell victim to an attack by pirates a few days ago while en route from Kaelops, and sunk. Regrettably, my customary source for these essentials has thus been disrupted. That is why you are here." Lasceaux tossed a gnawed human hand upon the stone floor then, like a dilettante, picked through the remaining parts before selecting another morsel. "As a natural philosopher of no mean skill," he boastfully continued, "I have discovered in my researches a method whereby these critical substances, inherent in the terrestrial body, may be sublimated and extracted for use as uncorrupted, specific elements. Because bodies in this plane are composed of much finer substances than yours, they are useless to me. I require a physical body like those found in your world. The quantities that I obtain from your body will permit me to continue my work until I can reestablish a more regular source for them."

Smith was stunned by his captor's insouciance. Moreover, based on the displays of his power he'd already suffered, he entertained little doubt that Lasceaux was fully capable of making good on his claims.

The alchemist added, "But in order to provide me with satisfactory materials, you must replenish your weakened body and increase your physical stores." He was silent for a few minutes while he picked the flesh from a bone. "Now you know what purpose I have in mind for you," he concluded as he again wiped his mouth on his dirty sleeve. He turned on his perch to face his captive who, though continuing to suffer a burning sensation throughout his body, had finally managed to drag himself into a sitting position, where he slumped against a craggy wall.

"Why did you choose me in particular?" Smith manage to croak.

"You or someone else...it was a matter of supreme indifference to me. Under the circumstances, it was less irksome to bring you here rather than one of your fellows. There is nothing exceptional about you."

Smith cautiously shifted his uncomfortable position. As he did so, he noticed a piece of fruit from his earlier meal still lying on floor nearby. He cautiously retrieved it with his foot, tucking the fruit in the folds of his clothing.

"I guess that means I'll not be returning home," he said, flatly.

"There will be nothing left of you *to* return, fool! Every aspect of your whole will be sublimated and consumed within the week."

Smith curled up on the floor and yawned extravagantly beneath Lasceaux's hooded gaze. He closed his eyes.

"You may rest now, but there will be food here when you awaken. I grow weary of indulging you. You will then eat or suffer my wrath," the alchemist threatened.

But Smith was already oblivious to the diatribe, sleeping the sleep that comes from knowing one's mind.

IV

When he awoke half an hour later, he was alone. Smith trained himself, during his years as a soldier, to sleep predetermined lengths of time when occasion demanded. Occasion demanded it now.

Although weak from hunger, he rose softly to his feet, where he paused to steady his whirling head. Now: he must begin work quickly in order to complete his task before Lasceaux returned.

Acting as swiftly as his enervated condition permitted, Smith moved to a messy table upon which he had earlier noticed a scattering of bottles containing various powders. There! The yellow one.

Smith removed its glass stopper and cautiously sniffed its contents: sulfur. He turned next to one of the small lamps that languidly flickered in its receptacle in the stone wall; its weight told him that it brimmed with fuel. Extinguishing the flame with dampened fingers, he locked open the lamp's cover and poured its warm odiferous oil into one of the alchemist's pestles. Into it Smith hastily dumped the yellow powder from the bottle. Grabbing a mortar, he began to grind the two substances into an oily paste.

Carrying the mortar and pestle, he retrieved the piece of fruit he had earlier secured and rapidly began to smooth the glistening pastiche across its surface.

Feverishly scooping out the last bits of paste from the dish, Smith tossed the pestle into an unlit corner of the cavern and carefully smoothed the fruit's golden sheathing. The rough texture of its skin helped the mixture cling better than he anticipated.

Smith carefully wrapped the fruit in his clothing, then freely rearranged the jumble of beakers, flasks, and dusty parchments that littered the rough table. Just as he finished, the alchemist drifted in silently from his mission of procuring dinner. Smith noted thankfully that Lasceaux was carrying a platter of fruit, rather than one of offal.

"What are you doing!" the latter shrieked upon seeing Smith standing near his equipment.

Trying to appear as insouciant as possible, Smith glanced up and airily replied, "I thought you flattered yourself the greatest natural philosopher in the world." He was desperately attempting to keep his outward demeanor calm...inwardly he was fearful beyond measure. "I'm surprised that you should be ignorant of the writing of the great initiate, Eirenaeus Philalethes." Smith hoped that by glibly using the name of one of the most renowned alchemists in history he would immediately capture Lasceaux's attention.

The alchemist abruptly dropped his tray and it clattered to the floor. "Get away from my work, cretin!" he spat.

Knowing that his captor would immediately reach for his burning powder, Smith swiftly responded,

"If you hope to ever produce the Philosopher's Stone, hear me out. If you raise even a finger against me, I promise that you will labor fruitlessly forever."

Lasceaux, taken aback by his prisoner's brazenness, was undisguisedly impressed. Smith noted this and paused only a moment before continuing his performance.

"I assume you are familiar with the *Aureus Liber* of Philalethes. If so, you must know the important principles that are established in it," Smith cryptically said.

"Of course, I have read Philalethes," snapped Lasceaux. "I have never heard of the *Aureus Liber*, though, nor of the principles of which you speak." Despite his wariness, he was becoming intrigued.

Smith reached behind his back and produced his golden orb. "Obviously not, else you would have produced this long ago," he said as indifferently as he could.

An involuntary gasp escaped the lips of the alchemist. Even in the dim chamber, Smith could sense his entire demeanor abruptly change. The light from candles and oil lamps glittered seductively off the golden orb in his hand. Lasceaux moved eagerly forward to seize the prize.

"No! I created this lump of gold from your own materials, Lasceaux," Smith lied as he cached the coated orb in his clothing. "I'll not share it with a blundering poseur like you."

Lasceaux suspended his advance. Smith could discern his hooded visage malevolently assessing him.

"How did you accomplish this? I have been absent only a brief while yet, in that time, you have achieved what has eluded me for centuries," murmured the alchemist, unable to conceal his awe at Smith's apparent accomplishment.

"By employing the principles established by Philalethes in his *Aureus Liber*, of course," replied Smith. "You would do well to peruse Philalethes more attentively," he advised, though he had only moments earlier invented the fictitious title.

"I do not know from whence to obtain the book of which you speak. You will instead instruct me in the principles," commanded Lasceaux, whose avarice was already beginning to cloud his prudence.

"Why should I? I owe you nothing."

Lasceaux was silent for a few seconds, as if sizing up Smith. Then he spoke. "Tell me your secret principles, let me create such gold here for myself, and I shall return you to your proper place."

"Nice try. First, you tell me how to get back; only then will I impart the secret."

"You have already witnessed the potency of my skills," the alchemist bragged. "I could simply obliterate you at this moment and take your gold."

Smith slowly nodded. "Yes, that's quite true...if you're an even bigger fool than you appear to be. If you kill me, you'll have to be content with the trifling amount of gold I created while you were gone." He paused and smiled craftily. "If you release me, though, I will impart my secret of producing incalculable amounts of gold. I leave the decision to you."

Lasceaux was grim as he contemplated Smith's proposal.

"I will not return you whence you came, as your secret may turn out to be a deception...having freed you, it will prove difficult, notwithstanding my redoubtable skills, to retrieve you." The alchemist paused. "Instead, I will release you into *my* world, where I can easily locate you should your information prove counterfeit."

Smith found it difficult to conceal his disappointment at this response, though he realized that Lasceaux was unlikely to liberate him unconditionally.

"Agreed," he responded. "As soon as I'm free of you, I'll write down the key to my secret and place it where you can easily find it. If you attempt to follow me, though, I'll tell you nothing and you'll labor forever without success in your vain search for the Stone. Now, release me immediately."

"Bear in mind your obligation, also," cautioned Lasceaux. "Should this be a trick and your gold prove specious, I will locate you without any difficulty. No one trifles with the mighty Lasceaux with impunity," he asserted in an effort to recapture his dignity after being schooled by his own prisoner.

The alchemist walked to a table and, after a few moments of searching, located a divining rod, slate, and stylus.

"This staff will lead you to the outside world," he said, indicating the divining rod. "Once there, write down the means of producing your remarkable Philosopher's Stone on this slate, that I, too, may make such gold. After you have done, leave these implements, along with your golden orb, in the branches of the large Teasel tree you will see nearby. These are my conditions; if you fail to satisfy them, your life will be forfeit," Lasceaux solemnly concluded.

Irrespective of the fact that Smith fully comprehended the potential deadly consequences of his ruse, he reasoned that whatever fate ultimately befell him could certainly be no worse than the lethal destiny he knew was otherwise imminent. Indeed, while he had rendered a reasonably convincing performance, he was greatly surprised that his captor had been so quickly fooled. It was clear that Lasceaux was far greedier than wise.

"I will do as you wish, except that I intend to keep the gold that I have already produced, should I need it to barter with later on," Smith coolly replied. He could ill afford to surrender to the alchemist his spurious gold, thereby immediately revealing his deception. "With my formula you will easily be able to produce a thousand times as much gold for yourself."

Lasceaux stepped away from the table containing the divining rod, slate, and stylus. Confirming that his ersatz gold was secure in his ragged clothing, Smith cautiously made a wide arc to retrieve the three items. Grasping the two handles of the divining rod, Smith made a final, shuddering survey of his dungeon and its detestable lord, then stepped firmly into the void beyond the gloomy laboratory.

***

Smith rested in the cool darkness. Although he realized that it would not profit the alchemist to harass or betray him, he nevertheless strained to hear evidence of pursuit. Neither the sight nor the sound of pursuing footsteps disturbed the ebon air. The blackness that enveloped him was absolute, defying all of Smith's efforts to orient himself. The only thing that was clear was that his exodus was taking much longer than he'd hoped, though Smith was unable to determine exactly how great a distance he'd traveled in the darkness. The divining rod which he tightly clutched provided the only direction in the featureless void, tugging him inexorably farther and farther into the abyss. It seemed that he had already been walking for hours, plodding dully as the beckoning wand urged him onward. Now, he rested on the cold floor while the divining rod danced in his hands, insisting that he continue without respite. Hunger gnawed at Smith.

Struggling to his feet, he again yielded to the importuning rod and resumed plodding forward once again.

What seemed a fortnight later found Smith still trudging doggedly onward, stumbling over the uneven floor. Now, however, the stagnant air started, almost imperceptibly, to take on a less morbid hue. Beginning slowly, the atmosphere began to grow clearer, enabling Smith, after a little while, to view his surroundings.

He could see that he was in a large cave with rugged, naturally hewn walls and a looming ceiling. Numerous crevices branched from the central chamber, leading to unexplored grottos, and Smith was thankful to have the divining rod to indicate the proper route. The floor of the huge cave was worn smooth, as if by the action of water or the passage of innumerable feet over immense ages.

Smith abruptly stopped in his tracks as he stumbled upon an unexpected and totally unheralded sight.

Before him on the wall, about 30 inches from the floor, was etched a petroglyph, unmistakably the deliberate creation of an intelligent hand. Done primarily in crimson and black, the symbol also contained lesser amounts of other tints, several of them unlike anything Smith had ever seen, and was in the shape of an irregular octagon. The sight of the cryptic etching so surprised Smith that he unconsciously cast a swift glance about in the expectation of catching sight of its covert designer. He saw nothing but the dim and lifeless interior of a cave.

After stopping to examine the puzzling hieroglyph, Smith acceded to the persistent tug of the divining rod and resumed his passage through the increasingly lambent tunnel. He had scarcely proceeded twenty feet when another drawing was made manifest. Like the first, this one boasted a host of unclassifiable colors but, unlike the first, was in the shape of a quasi-hexagram.

Pausing only momentarily this time, Smith quickened his step. Sensing that the mouth of the cave was nearing, he hastened along the rocky corridor. The passageway was now covered with inexplicable etchings, as well as a series of shallow, empty, hollows excavated into the walls. The cave was now quite light, enabling Smith to view the phenomena with ease.

It was then that he saw the bones.

On the floor beneath a small recess they lay in a careless heap. Broken and dirty, their delicacy reflected a creature of diminutive size though their provenance was impossible to determine. The only thing Smith could definitely ascertain is that the unsettling jumble was clearly not of recent origin. It was at that moment that it dawned on him.

The bones, the drawings, the hollows...he was traversing a catacomb, but a catacomb for very small people or children. Smith had toured the catacombs of Paris and Rome and finally recognized the conclusive evidence all around him. The disordered bones and the many empty hollows bore grim testimony to the source of the alchemist's larder over many years.

Although Lasceaux previously referred to his dealings with a Kaelopian trader, Smith was otherwise utterly ignorant regarding the existence of other denizens beyond the confines of the alchemist's laboratory. Smith was none-the-less heartened to discover that, whatever their nature, the other inhabitants clearly practiced funereal customs. They must therefore possess some measure of religion and culture. Whatever their nature, they could scarcely be more barbaric than Lasceaux.

Because of the brightness now permeating the charnel, Smith was able to progress confidently. Everywhere he looked his eyes were met by more scatterings of bones, more etched fetishes, and more and more tenantless crypts. Almost oblivious to the tugging of the divining rod in his hands, he still avoided the unlit thresholds leading to other galleries that periodically opened off the main corridor and stuck to the well-worn passage beneath his feet.

***

After spending an eternity wandering Orpheus-like through the underworld, Smith finally disembogued the catacombs. Stepping apprehensively beyond the cavernous entrance, he viewed for the first time the world through which he must not only elude Lasceaux, but from which he must also return home.

V

The entrance to the cavern was sheltered by an immense cromlech, chipped and lichened but of indeterminate age, and located in a sloping coppice of evergreen trees. Between their velvety limbs Smith glimpsed far below a bucolic lowland of wooded hills and glens, as well as the gleam of a distant river. Not far from where he stood beneath the overhanging dolmen grew a gnarled tree with an immense trunk and lavender tendril-like leaves. Suspended from its branches were clusters of fruit like that he had eaten while a prisoner and which had provided the core for his gilded orb. This tree, he concluded, must be the Teasel tree in whose limbs he was to deposit his gold-making secret.

Withdrawing the stylus and slate from his ragged clothes, Smith sat down, rested his back against the ancient tree, and began to write. Ten minutes later he laid aside his pen and scrutinized his composition. It said: combine in a pestle seven parts oxia of nitre, one-part philosophical mercury, and three parts cinnabar. Calcinate these together until all that remains is a black dust lining the sides of the vessel. Into this residue grind an egg of kermesite and sublimate through distillation, adding exactly 32 drams of virgin's milk. The bitter orange powder that results is that which you seek.

Smith hoped that although simplistic, his spurious formula, gleaned from a casual acquaintance with Medieval alchemy, would prove sufficiently enticing that Lasceaux would spend time experimenting with it. The later Lasceaux realized that he had been duped, the better.

Smith collected his materials and rose slowly to his feet. He was exhausted, sore, and hungry, but the region beyond promised both respite and wholesome sustenance. Flinging the divining rod into the brush, Smith placed the stylus and slate in an overhead cleft of the massive Teasel tree. He began to carefully pick his way down the sylvan hillside toward the lowlands. Though choosing what appeared to be the easiest route, dense grass and copious florae on the lower slope soon began to hinder his already tedious descent until, painfully breaking through a particularly large clump of lantana, he chanced upon a narrow path. Clear of impediments and bordered by tiny wild flowers, it cut lazily through the forest in two directions, obliquely leading both uphill and also descending to the valley beyond.

Hesitating only momentarily, Smith turned to follow that section of the trail leading downward, around a copse of slender, green-barked, trees. Only a few yards beyond, Smith was delighted to encounter a large tree, its branches heavy with small crimson fruit resembling cherries, virtually overhanging the path. He recklessly grabbed the glossy spheres, suddenly ravenous at the sight of food, and crammed them into his mouth. He ate until he vomited the syrupy fruit, then ate more until he was sick. Finally satiated from his injudicious repast, Smith stepped from the trail and laid in the deep, cool grass beneath the tree. In seconds he was asleep.

***

It was nearly dark when he awoke. Across the path in a small yew tree two mourning doves were softly preparing their roost for the night. They were the first evidence of animal life Smith had encountered since his exodus from the alchemist's lair. He rose shakily to his feet and, finding himself hungry again, began nibbling at the fruit that overhung the path. Besides stemming his hunger, the copious juice also served to satisfy his thirst.

Because daylight was rapidly diminishing, Smith decided it prudent to conceal himself as best he could in the luxuriant grass and spend the night where he was. Accordingly, he retreated back to his hideaway near the base of the tree and promptly fell asleep once again.

***

"Ooomph!"

Something heavy smashed into Smith's chest as he slumbered. Leaping up, his heart pounding, he looked wildly about for the source of the assault on his quiescence. Smith saw nothing out of the ordinary.

He dropped to his knees and frantically began searching the area with his hands in an effort to find the object that had struck him. He encountered nothing except grass and soil.

"Ow!" He was flattened as yet another object drove him to the ground. Smith rolled onto his back, dumbfounded. He feared that Lasceaux had discovered he'd been conned and had already managed to track him down.

Smith looked straight up into the branches of the overhanging tree.

Seated midway down one of the tree's gnarled limbs was a diminutive, rotund man dressed in a green loin cloth and sporting a woven brown cape. Bearded and with long plaits of dirty white hair on his head, the figure malevolently surveyed the astonished Smith with baleful eyes.

"Hello!" stammered the latter, stupidly, not knowing what else to do but feeling obligated to do *something.*

The stoic figure did not verbally respond. Instead, he summarily launched himself from his perch and crashed solidly into Smith's chest before his bewildered victim could scramble out of harm's way. Smith frantically attempted to grab his assailant but the little man abruptly vanished into the long grass.

Smith lay quietly for a few seconds, then fearfully sat up and looked about, bracing himself for another attack. All was still.

He clambered to his feet and undertook a cautious exploration of the immediate area, hoping to discover the identity of his assailant. Although he'd been sound asleep when initially attacked, he was fully awake now and had no doubt that he'd actually *been* attacked. *Why* the assault had occurred, and whether the man was one of the alchemist's minions, Smith couldn't guess.

Feeling it essential to promptly decamp in order to prevent further attacks, Smith rapidly bound in his garment as much fruit as it could hold. Returning to the path, he weighed which direction to take. Concluding that it was essential to put as much real estate between himself and the alchemist's lair as rapidly as possible, Smith decided to simply resume the downhill route he'd undertaken the previous day, though he had no idea where it ultimately led. But, he thought to himself, all paths must lead *somewhere*. First and foremost, Smith had to distance himself from Lasceaux's wrath, which he knew would not be long in coming.

Smith apprehensively resumed his sojourn down the narrow trail, past groves of what he recognized as aspen trees and thick clumps of magnolia. Ferns and pale mushrooms grew lavishly in the moist ground where sunlight was blocked by the canopy of trees, and everywhere a carpet of dense grass cooled Smith's bare feet. The sky was crystal blue, interrupted only by distant masses of cumulus clouds rearing themselves into billowy citadels.

As he walked, Smith nibbled steadily at the cache of cherries swathed in his clothing. When his stained hand encountered the decoy he'd employed to deceive the alchemist, he paused to examine it. The fragile sheathing that coated the simulacrum was cracked and disintegrating. Anticipating no further use for the ersatz golden orb, Smith casually tossed it into the undergrowth.

Turning his attention back to the trail, Smith was startled to find the path blocked by another dryadic figure resembling the being he had the previous misfortune of meeting.

Garbed in a coarse jerkin, the bearded nisse stood about three feet tall and possessed feathery hair, a prodigious nose, and enormously elongated ears. Like his earlier counterpart, he bore a sour expression.

Smith stopped in his tracks while the elemental, who stood with arms crossed barely a dozen feet in front of him, surveyed him with disdain.

"Hello," Smith nervously greeted, slowly extending his arms laterally outward in a primitive token of non-aggression. "I mean you no ill. My name is Arthur Smith."

The gnome spoke in a voice so aged that it scarcely befitted a being of such tiny stature. "From whence come ye, and why?"

Startled at the little man's unexpected loquaciousness, Smith responded eagerly, though warily. "I am lost. I was abducted from my home but managed to escape my captor. I mean you no harm." He was hesitant to speak too freely to the enigmatic being since he knew neither its motivations nor its allegiances.

"Who was he who abducted thee?"

"An alchemist named Lasceaux."

At the mention of this name the elemental grew visibly affrighted. "Whom do ye serve?" he asked, suspiciously.

Uncertain as to the appropriate response to this challenge, and fearful of crossing his inquisitor, Smith replied with great circumspection, "I am beholden to no man."

"Serve ye the alchemist, who be no man?" demanded the gnome.

Sensing the dryad's antipathy toward Lasceaux, Smith emphatically declared, "No! The alchemist seized me from my home and made me his prisoner. I was lucky to have escaped from his cave before he killed me!"

"Why, then, do ye bear the alchemist's garments, which offend our noses and insult our wits?"

"He gave me these to wear. I had no choice."

The agrestic dwarf remained motionless for several seconds as he silently assessed Smith, who uncomfortably shifted his weight from one foot to the other. The skin on the back of his neck baked in the sun. Smith's stomach growled.

Presently, the gnome spoke. "Ye must prove what ye claim." Without waiting for a response, he produced from his pocket a large clay pipe and, without troubling to light it, began to puff on it contemplatively, producing great clouds of fragrant smoke.

Smith looked beyond the impassive figure and saw plodding up the path toward them a shaggy creature the size of a large dog, led by another of the seemingly ubiquitous gnomes. The animal's flaccid dewlap flopped this way and that as it walked and two short, fluted horns sprouted from its head. The gnome

Without waiting for a response, he produced from his pocket a large clay pipe and, without troubling to light it, began to puff on it contemplatively, producing great clouds of fragrant smoke.

leading it was clothed in the same rustic manner as his companion.

As he approached, the newcomer cheerfully hailed his comrade, "Holla, Milo!"

"Holla, Bolander. Life, prosperity, health," responded Smith's interrogator as he turned to greet the new arrival.

"Hath the intruder discovered himself to thee?" inquired the latter as he drew near. It was clear that

Bolander was having a difficult time keeping his meandering burden in tow, as he was constantly yanking on the animal's lead rope in an effort to keep the beast on track. As they arrived abreast of the unmoving Milo, it placidly wandered off the path and contented itself with browsing on a patch of yellow wild flowers.

"Indeed, but his claims are yet proved," replied Milo. He turned to Smith. "This animal," he said, indicating the creature that was happily grazing nearby, oblivious to all, "is a dremloch. It possesses the ability to distinguish truth from untruth. What ye must do is grasp the dremloch's tail unobserved. If ye speak truthfully the dremloch will remain mute. If ye are deceiving me it shall cry out loudly and betray thy deception."

Smith observed the animal's luxuriant tail as it ambled in the direction of another patch of flowers; its tail was so long that it dragged the ground and was matted with bits of grass and twigs. Bolander tugged at its leash and it stubbornly followed him out of sight into a thicket of alder trees. In a moment the gnome returned alone.

"The dremloch is secure," he announced.

Milo motioned for Smith to follow Bolander into the alder copse. Smith dubiously complied by stepping into the thick grass that bordered the path, adopting an awkward gait in order to avoid out-distancing his diminutive guide. Milo silently brought up the rear. Bolander struggled to stay in the lead because of Smith's much longer legs. No one spoke.

Smith considered ignoring the imperious demands of his rather comical captors by simply walking away. But, because he knew nothing about them, or the extent of their powers, he felt such a move unwise. He would forebear for the time being.

Entering the thicket, the trio immediately encountered the opening to a subterranean cavern, partially obscured by an abundant growth of ferns and tall grass.

Bolander stepped to one side and said to Smith, "Immediately inside this grotto is tied the dremloch; grasp its tail in both hands. It shall be the final arbitrator." Although Smith had no intentions of allowing the beast to decide his fate, he none-the-less nodded and stooped to enter the cave. The dremloch would decide his next move for him.

The interior of the cavern was nearly as cramped as its entrance augured. It extended several yards into the terrain before its jagged ceiling curved downward to join its rough floor. Smith had to proceed hunched over to keep from banging his head. The placid animal stood with its head lowered near the back of the cave.

Glancing about to make certain he was alone, Smith stepped to the motionless animal, which appeared to have fallen asleep. Reaching down, he sheepishly grabbed its thick tail with both hands. The dremloch did not stir. Smith did not know exactly what else the ritual required of him, but feared annoying the beast by hanging onto its tail too long. Accordingly, he gently released it while the homely animal continued to doze.

Smith turned and strode from the cave. The two gnomes stood immediately outside, as grim as before, only Milo was now holding in his hand a small object.

"Seat thyself and extend thy hands," he commanded, pointing to the ground in front of him. Smith complied then limply extended his hands, wondering how much longer the farce was going to continue.

"We shall now see how truthful thou truly art," Milo informed him. It was clear that the object in his hand was the bulb of some variety of plant. The gnome held it over Smith's outstretched hands and began squeezing mightily with his knotted fingers until clear sap began to run between them and drip onto Smith's hands. After a considerable quantity of the juice had glazed them, Milo ceased his efforts and dropped the crushed bulb onto the ground.   A pleasant, cooling sensation enveloped Smith's skin.

The two dryads each made a half-step forward and intently scrutinized Smith's outstretched hands which, to his astonishment, began to turn bright red beneath their glistening coating of sap. At the sight of this, the intense little men broke into wide smiles. Smith slowly lowered his hands.

"Because thy hands become as blood when touched with the flow from the Xanthus root, it is manifest that, unwatched, ye truly grasped the tail of the infallible dremloch. By this, it is evident that thou fearest neither censure nor reproach concerning thy relationship with the alchemist.   We accordingly offer our sincere friendship and heartfelt apology for the unhappy reception ye suffered," Milo gravely pronounced as Bolander beamed. "Ye can be assured our hostility reflected only our unease that ye served Lasceaux, our enemy, whom we greatly dread. We beg thee to accompany us to our home, where ye shall be received as   our esteemed guest. There thou mayest sup and take thy ease for as long as ye wish." So saying, he and Bolander gently helped Smith to his feet.

"What of the dremloch?" asked Smith, looking toward the mouth of the cavern.

"The dremloch's home is the forest," replied Bolander. "The beast is content.   Ye need suffer no anxiety for its welfare."

But Smith was still thinking of the contentedly dozing beast as the trio returned to the path and began to tramp toward the apparent dwelling of his new hosts.

VI

The room thronged with dryads. Every spare foot of floor appeared to be populated and the overflow occupied niches excavated in the walls, from which vantage the proceedings could be viewed unobstructed. Smith was seated on a woven grass mat, having awakened only a short time before, and was awaiting with great anticipation the imminent arrival of King Gob, ruler of the forest community. Bolander and Milo, Smith's de facto *valets de chambre*, informed him that the king had hastened to see him immediately after his arrival, but finding him asleep, quietly withdrew, refusing to disturb Smith's repose. Since initially entering the metropolis of the gnomes, for it could truly be called nothing less, Smith had been treated with the utmost deference by its denizens.

The city itself was situated less than a quarter-mile from the point Milo initially accosted him on the path and, Smith estimated, probably about three miles from Lasceaux's den. The trail leading to the city traversed a veritable Arcadia, where moss-girded trees sheltered tangled masses of fragrant orchids, and bowers of honeysuckle canopied fields of silken grass and oceans of wildflowers. As they progressed, Smith caught glimpses of the gaudy plumages of tiny, bejeweled birds as they flitted amongst the foliage, and briefly glimpsed the rusty coat of an elusive fox as it darted across the path in front of them.

Unobtrusive, indeed, unrecognizable at first, the gnomes' hidden city was entered through a fissure in an enormous massif of rose quartz, the fracture occasioned by the growth of an incalculably ancient tree that grew directly through the boulder.

Milo was the first to reach the portal when they finally arrived. Without hesitation, he scrambled through it to the subterranean metropolis below.

Smith cautiously peered into the unlit hollow between the boulder and the massive tree trunk. The outline of a shallow step was worn into the contiguous rock and he gingerly squeezed his frame along the tree's colossal girth and placed his foot on it. Smith stretched his leg into the dark recess below, searching for another toehold, until his foot encountered a second step. Depending on how deep the subterranean cavern extended, the tree must be of extraordinary height, Smith thought, as he cautiously inched his way downward. Above him, Bolander enthusiastically urged haste. Milo presumably waited for them somewhere in the darkness below.

Smith maintained firm grip on the tree truck as he cautiously descended into the murky recesses below. After what seemed an eternity of cautious descent, Smith finally entered a great shimmering hall via what was basically its ceiling. Immediately after his feet touched the rocky floor, he was besieged by a throng of excited dryads, not excluding the jubilant Milo, all of whom pressed eagerly forward to see the colossal foreigner who had blundered so suddenly into their midst.

Since his arrival in their city, Smith had learned that Bolander and Milo, indeed, all the little people, hated and feared Lasceaux. The alchemist plundered the sanctified graves of the gnomes' ancestors in order to feed off their remains. When Smith recounted how he had tricked the alchemist into freeing him, the elementals delighted in hearing how easily the venal alchemist had been duped. Only four days previously, Lasceaux had emerged from his lair to ensnare two of their kind who were visiting the ancestral burying place to pay homage. These he spirited into his den, for he preferred fresh kills to carrion. A companion of the two victims, who managed to escape, witnessed their abduction and returned much saddened that he was unable to save his comrades, who had, only moments before, boasted that they were invulnerable to the alchemist's powers. It was only then that Smith realized the origin of the platter of fresh meat that Lasceaux had offered him. Provided they did not fall victim to one of the alchemist's relentless ambushes, the gnomes were generally able to elude him. All dryads possess the ability to move with great swiftness when necessary, and it is this capability that represented their greatest defense. Indeed, it enabled Robert, the gnome who had previously launched the attack on Smith from the boughs of the mazzard tree, to vanish with such astonishing celerity.

"Why do you find it necessary to venture so close to the alchemist's laboratory, thereby putting yourselves in harms way?" Smith asked.

"Our fathers came to this land countless generations ago; exactly how long no one may hazard. Here they settled and in the nearby Nustazien Highlands, where the alchemist later established his lair, did they inter their honored dead. The prodigious dead of innumerable generations hath subsequently been interred there, a practice predating Lasceaux and as old as the Highlands themselves. It is perilous to spurn such a venerable tradition."

Smith questioned his hosts on this and a multitude of other subjects as they joyously guided him through their subterranean city, through lofty halls illuminated only by glowing chunks of a material which, they informed him, was dug from the ground at certain auspicious locations. Through fan-vaulted rooms whose towering ceilings were supported by monolithic pillars of brilliantly painted limestone. Into vast galleries containing stone tripods ablaze with fires that emitted neither heat nor smoke, fueled with a special wood which was simultaneously consumed and renewed by the flames. Down sloping passages wherefrom individual kobold homes branched like buds from the willow shoot. And, with respect to Smith's many questions, they responded with directness and simplicity.

All whom he encountered were clad in simple woodland garb and bore the aspect of advanced years: the men invariably sporting beards and the women having creased and furrowed visages typically associated with sagacious dispositions.

"But where are your children?" Smith had inquired, noting their conspicuous absence.

"Our children are raised communally," Bolander explained, "and remain apart until such time as they are able to render service to our entire community."

Smith discovered that, in addition to the Spartiate character of their child-rearing, the gnomes possessed no definitive cultural history, instead relying for knowledge of their origins on cryptic allegorical stories verbally transmitted from generation to generation. They espoused no uniform religion or philosophical system, though they asserted a belief in a continuing existence following physical death. Their opinions regarding the nature of this postmortem state were vague and ill-defined, but none-the-less required elaborate burial rituals. Smith also ascertained that the gnomes possessed no knowledge of Kaelops, the apparent source of Lasceaux's alchemical materials, nor of any other region beyond their own.

As the elementals spoke, it became abundantly clear that the baleful alchemist had preyed upon them for many generations and that they held nothing in such contempt and dread as they did Lasceaux. All these things, and more, Smith learned after descending into the city of gnomes. Finally, having fully rested, dined on an assortment of fruits, nuts, and nectars, and changed from his rotten clothing into a sweet-smelling flaxen robe, he eagerly awaited the arrival of King Gob.

There occurred a spontaneous hush throughout the prodigious hall. Smith strained to see across the crowded room as a gnome with trimmed hair and beard emerged from one of the tunnels that branched from the main chamber like the spokes of a wheel. The king's arrival prompted huzzahs and excited exclamations from his animated subjects. He spryly walked through the gathering, frequently stopping to speak with a particular individual, laughing uproariously all the while, until a few moments later he stood beside Smith.

Although Smith attempted to rise in a demonstration of respect, King Gob placed a gentle hand on his shoulder and bade him stay seated. In this manner he was virtually the same height as his guest and could address him the more easily. In his hands the king held a carved box of aromatic black wood.

"Warmest salutations on behalf of myself and my people," he greeted Smith in a jovial voice. "We wish thee life, prosperity, and health. I am Gob and thou art welcome here, where ye will find sanctuary and friendship for as long as thou wish." The king extended to Smith the box in his hands.

Opening the box, Smith discovered a ruby as dark and lustrous as the blood of the gyrfalcon. Noting his guest's stunned reaction, King Gob smiled and said, "'Tis is a gift from us to thee, serving both as an apology for our initial inhospitality and a token of perpetual friendship henceforth."

"I have done nothing to warrant such an exquisite gift," Smith protested. He gently closed the box and attempted to return it to his host.

"Thy presence among us is sufficient. We have done no more than what we would expect of another. Furthermore, our joy is multiplied because of the cleverness thou displayed in order to cozen our great enemy, a feat but rarely accomplished." This observation was punctuated by enthusiastic murmuring that rippled through the crowd.

Uncertain as to how he should respond, Smith said, "I am moved by your kindness, but cannot accept such a gift...its value far exceeds anything I have done."

King Gob beamed. "Thou art a stranger to our land, and charmingly ignorant of our ways." He directed a broad and knowing wink to the assembly at large, prompting several of his subjects to chuckle indulgently. "I therefore decree that a grand fete be celebrated in honor of thy presence among us, and that the revelry continue unabated until thou direct otherwise. I further decree that thou art invited to reside with us here, as our honored guest, for as long as thou desire, that thou mayest become fully acquainted...." The remainder of his words were rendered inaudible by the exclamations of delight that surged through the crowd.

The king leaned closer to Smith's ear. "Come with me," he instructed. Gob reached forward and grasped Smith's shoulder with an iron grip, literally lifting Smith partially to his feet before they were inundated by the ebullient gathering.

Smith fully stood and followed Gob as he threaded his way through the excited assembly. He found it rather difficult going because of the throng that pressed about them, coupled with his host's diminutive steps. None-the-less, they managed to make their way through the great hall, to a corridor lined with ancient carved pilasters. Smith still held the box containing the gem stone.

"I wish to show thee something," smiled King Gob as they walked down the empty passageway, their slippers making no sound on a floor worn slightly concave down its center by the passage of millions of feet over eons. The diminutive king proceeded with a surprisingly brisk stride when unimpeded.

"How is it," inquired Smith, "that although your people are of small stature, these halls are so expansive?"

"The entire region hereabout is a warren of natural fissures and rocky caves. The corridor through which we are now traversing, for example, and, indeed, the capacious grottos that form our entire city, are the work of a beneficent nature. Because we have occupied these caverns since the world was fresh, these chambers currently possess an altogether different character than the rugged clefts originally discovered by our venerated ancestors." As he spoke, Gob gestured toward a floor worn smooth by constant passage, and to stone walls embellished with peculiar arabesques and colorful designs. "Over time, we have also excavated auxiliary passages to facilitate movement between the larger corridors, and to provide for private dwelling spaces. The shining stone, which illuminates us, is easily mined and enables us to occupy these caverns in perfect peace and safety.

"Don't you and your people fear an attack from Lasceaux? Surely, he must know that your people live here. What prevents him from attacking your home?"

"He has no cause. We have nothing to offer him, as far as he is concerned, except the flesh of our dead," King Gob contemptuously spat. "Lasceaux is not as formidable as he fancies and is sufficiently prudent to realize that a direct assault on our people would gain him nothing. Moreover, were he to venture too far from his lair he would render himself vulnerable to attack by us. He is therefore content to prey upon us from the safety of the shadows. Conversely, we dare not menace his sanctuary in the Highlands because he would destroy without compunction those who flatter themselves his equal. Thou seest, then, that we exist in a state of equilibrium: the alchemist unwilling to affect a pogrom against us, and we unable to affect his ruin."

"Would it be possible for your people to move to a new land, or to bury your dead elsewhere?"

"As the most trifling apprehension inexorably gnaws at one's serenity until the latter ultimately yields, so does the alchemist's presence erode the collective bliss that would otherwise be my peoples' lot. Even if what thou suggest were possible, the alchemist would remain to despoil and pollute all that exists. As for thy question, however, our revered histories counsel us that the Nustazien Highlands have cradled our dead since the first of us succumbed to the clay. Because the location of the caverns is auspicious our dead must be interred there for as long as we exist. Other locations are simply unsuitable, nor are we free to repudiate the rituals of our fathers. Calamity and ruin stalk those who ignore the voices of the past."

They continued to walk as the king said these things. When he concluded they found themselves at the mouth of another tunnel branching off the main corridor.

King Gob explained, "My people seldom come here because it is rather isolated and no purpose would be served by doing so. Here are kept such fruits of the soil as may please thee, deposited here over a thousand generations and utilized by my people as ornaments and trinkets." So saying, he stepped aside to allow Smith to stoop and enter the cramped passage.

The small corridor angled obliquely into the wall of living rock for only a few yards, then veered sharply left before opening into a spacious room not unlike the large central hall they had recently quitted and where, presumably, the festival in Smith's honor was still being celebrated in his absence.

Situated along the periphery of the room were censers ablaze with the peculiar flame which neither consumed any fuel, nor emitted heat nor spark. As he stepped across the threshold into the chamber, Smith was able to stand erect. And the spectacle that greeted him benumbed his eyes.

Heaped about the rough floor and scattered throughout the chamber were mountains of gemstones, large and small. Piles of emeralds, diamonds, rubies, and sapphires glittered in the fluttering light of the censers, while a plethora of topaz, tourmaline, chrysoberyl, turquoise, lapis lazuli, and moonstone contributed their own quieter hues to the riotous collection. Individual stones were indiscriminately jumbled into chaotic mosaics: the diamond gleamed from beneath mounds of jade and the turquoise reposed atop the sapphire. While some of the gems were in their rough, natural state, as many more were cut and polished to a perfect degree. The room presented a symphony of color and a tumult of the highest exquisiteness.

"My people enjoy turning these stones into household decorations," remarked King Gob, softly, as he stepped abreast of Smith. "Other than this type," he remarked as he walked over and plucked a luminous moonstone from the floor, "which we use to illuminate our city, their only value lies in the pleasure they afford in cutting and polishing them for their own, innate charms."

"Surely you must utilize these for trade. They are worth an incalculable amount, or certainly would be to others."

"Trade? We have no dealings with others, save our unwanted association with the loathsome alchemist. Because our land provides all our wants in abundance, we have no need of trade. But it is true that Lasceaux prizes these stones mightily and exhibits an abominable delight when he discovers them in the pockets of those he manages to ensnare. What the alchemist does with the stones we know not."

Smith suspected that the alchemist used the gems as a medium of exchange for materials he required in his laboratory work, but said nothing.

"How is it that you are acquainted with the alchemist by name?"

King Gob sighed morosely. "The alchemist sometimes lies in wait in the neighboring forest, hoping to abduct any who wander too far from the safety of our home. Those who do not remain in a state of constant vigilance he seizes for his larder. But Lasceaux is notoriously vain. The few who manage to escape tell us that the alchemist prattles endlessly about himself."

"Does Lasceaux know that your people possess jewels in such quantity?"

"We think not. The alchemist believes that we merely chance upon them occasionally in the ground where we dwell. I fear that if he realized that we possessed such an abundance of his precious baubles, he would spare no effort to secure them. Regardless of its ultimate outcome, any such attack would certainly result in the deaths of many of my people. Because of thy resemblance to Lasceaux, at least in stature, we thought that ye also might prize the stones as dearly as he." The king chuckled, "It was thy unfortunate resemblance to the alchemist that led to thy initial unpleasant encounter with Robert, who chanced upon ye only by accident. We hope our gift will help to redeem us in thine eyes."

Smith squatted down before the little king and offered him his hand in friendship. Gob accepted it clumsily, unaccustomed to such a ritual, and reciprocated with an embrace that nearly cracked Smith's ribs.

"Come, let us return to the festivities," he enjoined.

VII

The great hall to which they returned vaunted an even greater congregation of elementals than previously. Smith feared that, in the prevailing overcrowding and confusion, some of the little beings would be smothered or crushed, but King Gob assured him that his concerns, though appreciated, were unwarranted.

Massive wooden tables occupying various areas of the crowded floor groaned beneath great stone bowls of wild berries and nuts. Other tables were topped with scores of ewers, filled to their brims with cooling libations. Still more tables labored beneath the weight of the profusion of fruits and carefully nurtured vegetables resting upon them. Though Smith could identify only cherries, carrots, and apricots, many other foodstuffs were there, as well. Along one side of the room a group of gnomes had formed a sort of ensemble and were intoning a lively song into the gala. Smith recognized Bolander plucking the strings of a balalaika, another strumming a lute, while yet another piped away on an ocarina, happily oblivious to all generally accepted concepts of musical harmony or melody. Additional elementals played various other instruments, all of which defied Smith's attempts to recognize.

Glancing down at his side Smith noted that his host had withdrawn from the folds of his garment a calabash, along with a woven bag of tobacco. Using a stubby finger, the king tamped a quantity of tobacco into the pipe's bowl, applied a glowing punk, and began to draw upon it with manifest contentment, producing billows of aromatic smoke.

Using a stubby finger, the king tamped a quantity of tobacco into the pipe's bowl, applied a glowing punk, and began to draw upon it with manifest contentment, producing billows of aromatic smoke.

Catching sight anew of their sovereign and guest whose recent disappearances had never-the-less done nothing to diminish the enthusiasm of the festivities, a few of the gnomes burst into what was evidently a traditional song of praise and respect, which was quickly taken up by the general company.

"I don't know how to thank you; I can't believe what has happened to me," Smith confessed to his host.

"How camest thou to be prisoner of the alchemist?" inquired Gob without taking his eyes off the revelers. A group of gnomes in the crowd were passing around a large demijohn, each saluting their king and guest before quaffing its contents, much to the delight of his fellows who laughed heartily as each participant drew the jug away from his lips, sputtering and wheezing. Across the room, other dryads danced to the music of Bolander's ensemble.

"He abducted me by way of magic from my home."

Expelling rich clouds of smoke, the king nodded, "Aye, the alchemist is no stranger to abduction. But where is thy home located? Surely not hereabouts for, other than the alchemist and those who sometimes call on him, we have never encountered anyone of thy singular appearance."

"There are no other men like myself around here?"

"Occasionally, beings resembling thyself, though peculiarly clad, troop through our land to the lair of the alchemist. They do not tarry long and their identity and business is a mystery to us," replied Gob, furrowing his brow as if in thought. Smith surmised these were likely the Kaelopian traders spoken of by the alchemist. "But where is thy home?" the king again inquired.

"I don't know where my home is, relative to this place," Smith confessed. "Nor do I know how to get there even if I *did*."

"Here, then, with us, shall be thy home. You are with friends."

Notwithstanding Gob's assurances, Smith was dismayed at the prospect of being marooned in a strange world to which he was distinctly ill-suited and yearned to return to his mundane province. Feeling present circumstances inappropriate for discussion of the matter, however, he begged leave of his host and picked his way through the convivial gathering to one of the tables ladened with platters of food. Taking an earthenware cup, he filled it with the strange liquid from one of the ewers. Smith's height afforded him an excellent vantage from which to observe the gaiety taking place at approximately the level of his waist, and he saw that King Gob had left their former position near the entrance of the room and was actively participating in something akin to an American square dance with some of his subjects. He also saw Milo threading his way through the revelers toward him and in a few minutes was warmly greeted by the latter.

"Hello, Milo. Will you join me in a libation?" invited Smith.

"Happily. How art thou enjoying thyself? I regret that thy size makes it impossible for thee to fully participate in the revelry, but be assured that everyone is enjoying a delightful time in thine honor. Whatever solace that may be I do not know, but perhaps ye can share in the merrymaking vicariously!" he laughed. Milo had already gulped down the contents of his cup and was pouring himself another drink. Smith had not yet sampled his.

"Milo, I confess that I feel rather strange, and not simply because of my size. Is it not odd that King Gob should decree a festival to honor one who is new to your community, and whose nature is so unlike your own? Moreover, of my history you know nothing, save that I lately escaped from the clutches of the alchemist. Other than that, you and your king know absolutely nothing about me. Yet you welcome me into your midst, bestow upon me a magnificent gift, and enjoy a holiday in my honor. Forgive my bluntness, but it all seems very gratuitous."

Milo drained his cup a second time, seated himself upon the floor carefully out of the way of particularly zealous dancers, and indicated that Smith do likewise.

After Smith had settled next to him, the gnome began. "I do not know from whence ye come, but wherever that is, thy kind must observe strange customs."

"How so?"

"Ye pour thyself refreshment, but do not drink it, preferring instead to hold it in thy hand. Ye thus deprive thy palate of a kindly and soothing balm. It is no wonder that thou dost not comprehend our delight at thine appearance amongst us." Milo gently chided Smith with a twinkle in his eye. In deference to his host, Smith obligingly sipped the rose-colored contents of his cup, finding the liquid to possess a mildly alcoholic sweetness reminiscent of cinnamon.

Milo continued, more seriously, "The acquisition of a new friend is always an occasion for celebration. It is doubly so when the friend is a stranger to the ways of another, for then there exists no opportunity for guile or deceit and his fidelity cannot be gainsaid. Such an occasion demands nothing short of a festival, for it is a rarity that kindred souls find themselves brought together by mere chance and no effort must be spared to mark the happy occurrence."

"But my appearance is so dissimilar to yours and so like that of your enemy, Lasceaux."

"The toadstool is lethal; the morel wholesome and salubrious. The former is avoided or sickness, even death, will result; the latter is much desired and consumed with delight, as well as for use in unguents and medicines. Though they superficially resemble one another, one brings evil, the other, good. So is it with everything."

"Surely, though, my appearance must provoke some unfavorable impressions in your people. Even so, no one has given the slightest notice of the spectacle I must present."

Milo smiled indulgently at the being who was apparently plagued with so much angst. "The mountainous ox does not spend its days mocking its brother, the frail egret, for it would be complete madness to do so. It is enough that the sharp-eyed egret's cries warn the near-sighted ox of the approach of the lion. To show its thanks the ox stirs up the insects which inhabit the grass beneath its ponderous hoofs, upon which the egret feeds. In this way the two friends assist each other. They were blessed with sufficient wisdom by our creator to understand that their differences work to the advantage of the other. If either spent the day ridiculing the other for being big and slow or small and weak, both would suffer."

"But of what use am I to you or your people? You have given me many things; what have I given you?"

"Thou hast given us the joy of thine friendship. We have returned it and have given ye sanctuary. A fair exchange has been made. I am truly surprised that the beings from whence thou comest seemingly do not observe this most fundamental verity of life, for if they did, ye would not be troubled by suspicions regarding our motives. Cast aside thy fears and misgivings, Smith. Take pleasure in the gala that thy friendship invokes and over which ye are our honored guest. The festivities shall continue for as long as ye deign, though I urge ye to temper thy convivial generosity with prudence, for I fear that we are a most festival-loving people and too much celebrating may well render us unable to perform on the morrow the chores which, unfortunately, dominate our lives!" This admonition was given in a half serious tone that prompted Smith to smile.

Standing, Smith took Milo's cup and refilled it, as well as his own. Taking a platter of voluptuous purple grapes from atop the table, he resumed his seat on the floor near Milo and placed the grapes between them.

Delighted by his guest's display of confidence and initiative, Milo popped one of the grapes into his mouth, jumped to his feet, and proposed to the assemblage, "Let us toast our new friend, Smith, whose ways are strange but who is an honored guest in our house!"

Upon this proposal the revelers began to applaud enthusiastically, at first those nearest the two then those in the extremities to whom the essence of Milo's toast was orally passed. The musical ensemble along the far wall, having now grown to include a total of a dozen performers playing as many instruments, struck up an arrangement which sounded cacophonous to Smith's staid ears, but which was greeted with enthusiastic approval by its diminutive hearers.

Milo grabbed Smith and easily pulled him to his feet, who was reminded of the tremendous physical strength of the gnomes. Quickly draining his cup of its enlivening contents, he followed Milo to the center of the expansive floor. At every step he was detained by dwarfs wishing to express personal pledges of friendship and esteem. Several of the small folk he recognized as having met while touring their city immediately after his arrival, but the greater number of them were new to him. This did not inhibit the latter from addressing him with extreme kindness and goodwill. Indeed, one of the elementals engaged in a drinking competition offered Smith the venerable demijohn which formed the focus of the contest, extolling him to sample its mysterious contents. Smith warily complied as the coterie of breathless gnomes watched.

Smith found the demijohn to contain a piquant liquid not unlike absinthe. Its alcohol content must have been considerable because, after sampling it, Smith was forced to inhale great wafts of air in order to cool his burning palate, a circumstance that sparked unrestrained mirth among his audience. Initially embarrassed, Smith also began to laugh, but the resulting tickle in his throat caused him to succumb to paroxysms of coughing which caused his audience to fairly shake with laughter at his hapless plight.

One of the gentle gnomes finally offered Smith a cup of water to ease his discomfort, while the whole company cheered his good humor and fortitude, the men embracing him at about thigh level and the women reaching to grasp his hands, as was their custom. Smith eventually made it to the middle of the floor where he was invited to participate in a promenade. Milo had since disappeared but, looking over the heads of the gnomes, Smith could see him far across the room filling his pockets with quantities of fruit from one of the tables. The ensemble along the wall had struck up yet another song, and having accepted an especially large and succulent apricot from an elfin merrymaker, Smith was whirled into the dance, the fruit clutched precariously in his mouth. The facility with which the tireless gnomes executed the steps of the complex dance amazed him and he was very glad when Milo, who finally returned with his trove of fruit, relieved him and allowed him to rest.

Munching his apricot, Smith threaded his way to a spot near the wall and betook himself to observing the activity whirling about him.

King Gob was across the room, laughing uproariously at an anecdote shared by one of his subjects. When he saw Smith he happily waved. Bolander was still animatedly playing his balalaika at the other end of the great hall, accompanied by the other musicians. Robert was dancing feverishly nearby, apparently inexhaustible. Most of the other gnomes throughout the room were also dancing, though several were helping themselves to the refreshments that occupied the tables covering every remaining foot of floor space. Invariably, he was warmly greeted by gnomes passing in his vicinity and his arms finally grew weary of returning their embraces.

And so passed the greater part of the night, in eating and dancing and singing and laughing, until completely fagged, Smith respectfully requested of King Gob a place to repose. The kindly patriarch bade all of his subjects retire and personally escorted Smith to private chambers wherein was placed a luxurious mattress filled with the softest of leaves and the most fragrant of petals. Bidding him good rest, the king withdrew and no sooner had Smith laid himself atop that nest than was he beckoned by Hypnos into his soporific domain, untroubled by all fears of inevitable pursuit or vengeance.

***

Upon awakening, Smith found a small basket of fruit placed on the floor near his mattress and, next to it, a basin of cool water and a stack of woven cloths. He rinsed and dried his face. Though somewhat invigorated, his head had not yet completely cast off the muddle from the previous night's revelry.

Smith sampled some of the fruit, discovering as he did so that he was hungrier than he might have supposed. A few minutes later Milo called softly from just outside the entrance to Smith's chamber. Smith rose and invited him in.

"I trust ye rested well," cheerfully greeted the elemental as he entered the room.

"I must have because I don't remember!" joked Smith. "Will you join me in breakfast?"

"I would fain do so and thank thee for thy kindness," said Milo as he plopped down on the floor and critically examined the basket of fruit before selecting a peach. Smith sat next to him.

Milo was clad as he had been since Smith had first encountered him in the forest, although how long a time that had actually been Smith could not accurately guess since he had been underground for the greater part of it and blind to the progression of the days. Moreover, he had slept several hours, as well. Milo still sported the same jerkin and neither his beard nor his hair had felt the bite of a razor for a considerable time.

"What will ye do today?" inquired the gnome as he munched on his peach.

"I don't exactly know. What *should* I do?"

"Since thou art our guest, ye should do whatever pleases thee," replied Milo matter-of-factly as he selected a plump pear from the basket.

Smith thoughtfully chewed an apple. Though the elementals had welcomed him warmly into their city and had treated him with the greatest kindness, he yearned for his rightful home. Unsure whether returning home was even possible, Smith was convinced none-the-less that his place was not with the elementals. Certainly, too, the alchemist by this time had realized that he had been made the fool and would surely undertake efforts to exact revenge. Given the proximity of their city to Lasceaux's laboratory, Smith's presence among the gnomes was likely to draw the alchemist's wrath upon them, too. Even if his hosts managed to defend themselves against the alchemist's retribution, Smith would still be no closer to his goal of returning home.

"Would it be possible for me to see King Gob?"

"Certainly," replied Milo as he popped an apricot into his mouth. Smith was much impressed by his guest's impressive appetite. "He awaits ye at thy leisure."

"Will you take me to him?"

"Of course." Milo scrambled up while Smith rose more slowly, his joints stiff and sore. Together they walked down a hallway that ran obliquely from the doorway leading to Smith's rooms. Smith continued to munch on his apple as Milo maintained a steady stream of commentary.

"Thence is Fob's domicile, and Alexander's and his wife's. There is Robert's and his wife's, and also Victor's and his," he said as he gestured about. In most of the doorways dryads were engaged in sweeping out their apartments with straw brooms or sitting on wooden benches sewing or repairing articles of clothing. Although clad in plain garments woven in subdued woodland hues, all the gnomes radiated robust health. As was usual, the passage was brightly lit by the marvelous glowing moonstones placed strategically along its length and which enabled the womenfolk to engage in the most exacting piecework in perfect comfort. As the two walked, Milo continued to indicate the homes of the various denizens of the city until they approached one which was of particular interest to him.

"This," he grandly announced as they paused before its tidy door, "is mine and my wife's." Smith met Milo's wife when he first entered the city and felt obligated to knock gently at the door to wish her a good day while Milo looked on approvingly.

In not much time the two reached the central chamber from which, Smith's previous tour revealed, all the other passages of the subterranean metropolis radiated and from the floor of which grew the immense tree he had descended hours or days ago. Its trunk was at least sixteen feet in diameter and its ancient gnarled branches, adorned with multi-colored berries, created a living canopy of verdure far overhead. Though he managed to conceal it, Smith was anxious to depart the gnomes, eager to rejoin the natural world above ground.

"We are tending the garden today," said Milo as they approached the tree staircase. "Gob will be glad to see thee."

Smith studied the soaring tree with consternation. Having paid little attention to it formerly, he'd forgotten just how large it was and how far it grew upward before emerging from the grotto into the daylight above.

Milo began scrambling up the stolid trunk with a confidence born of habit. After he had climbed about seventeen or eighteen feet, he turned, evidently expecting to see his guest close behind, but instead found him standing at the foot of the tree, looking up at him with obvious consternation.

"Come, Smith. I am sorry that this kindly tree provides the only means of access to the outside world. Her boughs will protect ye. Look and see where we have formed hand and foot holds through use over time; follow the path that the trunk bears and ye will be fine. Come now." Milo reclined against a limb of the tree with carefree abandon, one foot swinging into space, while he smoothed his unruly beard with his hand.

Smith warily approached the tree, placed the toe of his right foot in a small depression in the trunk formed by the accumulated pressure of uncounted dryad feet, reached up with his left hand, and boosted himself upward. Another toe-hold offered itself slightly above and to the left of the first, and Smith availed himself of it while grasping the rough bark of the tree with his hands. Though only four feet off the floor at this point, Smith's initial consternation at having to scale the juniper was swiftly abating, as he found that it was indeed easier than it looked.

In a few moments he rested alongside Milo, who grinned, "See how easy? Whatever may happen, ye can fall no farther than the floor!" With this assurance, the gnome resumed his ascent of the ancient tree with Smith picking his way, crab-like, behind him.

When they reached the great beetling limbs that overhung the gallery floor thirty feet beneath them, a wave of alarm suddenly gripped Smith because inadequate lighting at that height rendered it impossible to locate the toe and hand holds in the trunk. The glowing moonstones were far below, and such marginal illumination as reached him through the thick greenery was entirely insufficient. Moreover, the overhead fissure that cleft the boulder was so obscured by branches, and still so distant, that the small amount of exterior light it admitted was useless. Above him in the dimness Smith could hear Milo's noisy ascent.

Smith forced himself to slow his anxious breathing. With painstaking caution, he was able to proceed, even in the dimness, by delicately placing his hands and feet on slight irregularities in the thick bark. In so doing, he could thus find notches already in existence where generations of nameless elementals had done likewise. In the thickest branches overhead, Milo climbed steadily upward .

Presently, the gnome called down to him, "Smith! I am above ground and shall await thee."

He didn't respond but redoubled his efforts to reach the surface. In ten minutes time he managed to scale the remaining expanse of tree.

Pushing aside a dense cluster of branches, Smith was momentarily blinded by the glorious brilliance of the sun. He leaned back against the trunk of the tree and squinted his eyes against the dazzling sunlight.

The morning sky was startling blue with a flotilla of towering cumulus clouds sailing lazily along its azure expanse. Sitting atop the large quartz boulder whose hemispheres girdled the lofty tree he'd just ascended was Milo.

Seeing his charge emerge like an exhausted fledgling from its refractory egg, Milo smiled. "I feared ye had gotten lost in the boughs of the tree, my friend."

"Impossible!" Smith laughed. "I had no trouble finding my way upward simply by following the infernal racket that you made!" He gingerly picked his way along a limb of the tree toward the gnome. Easing himself onto the boulder next to Milo, Smith assessed the surrounding landscape with interest. "I'd forgotten how bright the sun can be," he idly remarked while looking about.

From his elevated vantage, Smith saw that the neighboring land was thickly wooded. Although the immediate vicinity had been cleared of encroaching verdure, dense forest crowded along the periphery of the cleared area. Low hills rose at a distance from the midst of the primeval woodland, dark and ominous with dense vegetation. Much closer, ash trees and graceful willows dominated the scenery, ivy and woodbine lacing along their branches. Brilliantly-plumaged birds flitted among the trees, the sunlight that caromed off their feathers causing them to appear more like animated jewels than living creatures. A fragrant haze suffused the warm air, suggesting that daybreak had occurred not long before. Above their heads the tree fanned out into a broad green canopy. Smith estimated the tree's aggregate height exceeded 150 feet.

Among the distant hills undoubtedly lay the Nustazien Highlands and, somewhere within them, the lair of the enraged alchemist whose vengeance would not be long in coming. Although all of the events that had recently befallen Smith seemed utterly surreal, he was none-the-less certain of the approaching wrath of Lasceaux, and his vulnerability to it.

"Where are the others?" he asked.

"This way," replied Milo as he began to scramble down the face of the boulder.

Milo reached the base of the rock and waited for Smith to join him. Smith jumped the last two feet to the ground and followed Milo along a trail leading into the glade.

"How many does it take to maintain your garden?" Smith asked as they walked.

"Because our garden provides for all of our people, it is extensive and requires the labor of no less than a dozen to properly maintain."

"What do the rest of your people do?"

"The womenfolk care for our homes. We menfolk cultivate the garden, forage for fruits and berries in the forest, work in the mines from whence we extract the stone that lights our city, gather the wood that warms us, and effect the general upkeep of our homes."

The two soon drew near the communal garden, which was located no more than 200 yards from the entrance to the dryads' subterranean home. The kibbutz occupied a clearing roughly 50 yards square, surrounded by evergreens and bounded on two sides by a small brook. As they approached, Milo called out a greeting to the several individuals who were busily engaged in weeding the plot on their hands and knees, or hoeing with rough implements.

"Hola, Milo! Hola, Smith!" exclaimed King Gob. "Life, prosperity, health!" He stood and slapped the dark, moist peat from his garment. Small bits of leaves and sticks clung comically to his beard and he instinctively reached up a muscular arm to brush them away.

"Good morning, Gob. I hope you are well today," greeted Smith.

"Very well, indeed, and how does the morning find thee, my friend? I trust ye rested well."

"I did, thank you. It's certainly a beautiful day. I told Milo that I'd nearly forgotten how wonderful the sun can feel."

"It does not do well to spend too much time beneath the soil, it is true. Doing so renders one insensible to the sublime delights of nature. Come, let us rest and discuss the matter that prompted thee to seek me out this morning." Smith was somewhat surprised at Gob's confidence that he, Smith, had a definite purpose in desiring to speak with him. Perhaps it was Smith's reserved manner that presaged it, or simply his general aspect but, in any case, Gob indicated a broad flat-topped rock at the periphery of the garden adjacent to the purling brook. They started toward the rock while the remaining elementals continued to work placidly.

It was only then that Smith noticed that Milo had disappeared.

"He will return shortly," Gob assured him when Smith expressed his surprise. As they walked along the perimeter of the garden toward the isolated rock, the laboring elementals they passed warmly greeted Smith and their king, who returned their salutations.

When they came upon a gnome who was earnestly hoeing the furrows of what appeared to be cabbage. Smith smiled broadly. "Hello, Robert," he said. "It's good to see you."

Robert grinned widely at the greeting and his eyes fairly sparkled. It was, Smith concluded, a vast improvement over the impression the gnome had made on him when he initially encountered him, glowering down from the limb of a tree.

"Holla, Smith. I share your pleasure at seeing thee. Have ye come to labor with us? If I were thee, I believe that I would find something more pleasurable to occupy my time," he laughed.

"Shhhh!" cautioned Smith with mock seriousness. "King Gob might put me to work if you don't hold your tongue!"

"Perhaps thou art right. I'll leave thee to thy business, then." Robert turned back to his work as Smith and King Gob resumed their stroll to the boulder, where they arrived after a few moments.

"What is troubling thee?" asked Gob, gently, as they seated themselves on its lichen-encrusted surface.

"King Gob, I wish first to express my thanks to you and your people for the many kindnesses you have shown me. Without your generosity I would surely have fared very badly in your world, and I thank you most humbly." The small brook at their feet gurgled rhythmically through the thick grass that lined its marshy banks. The soft laughter and voices of the gnomes working in the garden floated over to them, only to become intermingled with the natural music of the flowing water. A tiny silver fish momentarily broke the surface of the stream near the boulder; its sudden appearance startled a brilliant yellow frog concealed in the grass near its edge and it jumped into the stream with a loud "plop".

"Ye are most welcome. Should ill-fortune befall any of us, we would not hesitate to enlist thy help, so ye see that we are making an investment in our own well-being as well as aiding a friend."

"I understand, but thank you none-the-less. I sincerely hope that I can repay your kindness."

Gob smiled and placed a gnarled hand on Smith's shoulder "Perhaps ye shall. For the nonce, thy friendship is adequate payment. Trouble thyself no more about it."

Smith sat in contemplative silence for a few minutes, staring into the water as it danced along its course. The edifying perfume of the garden's rich loam wafted about them and, although the golden sun warmed his skin, the breeze that whispered through the adjacent forest, causing the trees to sigh and creak, palliated its fierceness.

"King Gob," Smith slowly began, "I don't quite know how to couch this and sincerely hope that my candor doesn't offend you, but felt that I could speak openly and take counsel in your wisdom." He paused in an effort to gauge the king's mindset, but Gob was content to quietly listen. Smith therefore continued. "I long for the world I came from and, truthfully, where I belong."

The king smiled warmly. "Thou need not fear offense on my part, Smith. I am truly honored that ye should deign to trust in my counsel. Indeed, though I would fain not hear of thy desire to return to the world from whence ye came, I knew that such words would not be forestalled. Though I do not know what help we can provide to aid thy return, my people and I are at thy disposal.

"Thank you. My indebtedness to you increases, it seems, by the minute."

"Be thou assured that ye are not indebted to us, save to console us when we are troubled and shelter us when we are destitute, inasmuch as it lies within thy power to do so. This is an obligation that is owed by all to all, and reserved exclusively to none. Now, how can we help thee?"

"Both you and Bolander told me that your people are unaware of any other lands or peoples other than Lasceaux and the men who occasionally visit him."

"That is true. All that we require for our existence is located in this immediate area. A periodic trek to the Highlands to inter our dead comprises the limit of our peregrinations."

"Have you any idea where I might begin a search for a way back to my homeland? While the alchemist claimed to possess the ability to return me there, I dare not return to his laboratory. I am certain, moreover, that he must by this time be looking for me."

"Look there", said Gob as he pointed toward the top of a large pine tree some 200 feet distant. Smith followed his gaze and saw perched among the top-most branches of the tree a greyish bird about the size of a raven. Extending from the breast of the creature, however, were two boney arms ending in zygodactyl claws, these appendages being in addition to the dark grey wings folded neatly against the bird's sides. Even at a distance this unusual feature was unmistakable, nor had Smith ever seen such a bizarre creature.

Extending from the breast of the creature, however, were two boney arms ending in zygodactyl claws.

"It is called the Ansut. The alchemist traps and trains them to do his bidding because they are marvelously intelligent and can easily be taught to talk, as well. That one has been sitting and observing us all morning. No doubt the alchemist suspects that you are among us and sent the Ansut to reconnoiter. If he did not know for a certainty your whereabouts, he will shortly."

As the king spoke, the Ansut spread wide its wings and floated out of the tree. Plunging straight down, it swooped upward an instant before plummeting into the ground, then glided elegantly over the heads of Gob and Smith with its strange arms tucked against its breast. As it sailed overhead the singular creature craned its neck and carefully scrutinized them with baleful eyes before flapping silently in the direction of the distant, misty hills.

"I must obviously depart immediately," asserted Smith, "not only for my own safety, but for the safety of your people, too. I have no doubt that Lasceaux will attempt to punish you when he discovers that you aided me."

"No doubt," replied King Gob, calmly. "But our immediate concern is thy safe passage back to thine homeland. Though we have no direct knowledge of anything beyond our realm, we possess an old chart depicting other, distant lands and waters. The origin of this document is unknown, even to us, but that it is incalculably old is certain. Our histories tell us that it was fashioned by our nomadic fathers in the obscure past. Their tangible record has remained here, with us, since that remote time. Though I cannot testify to the correctness of the map because my people have never had occasion to utilize it, you may examine it. Perhaps it will provide some insight."

"Where is this chart?" Smith asked, excitedly.

"Milo will return with it presently." No quicker than Gob had uttered these words than the elemental appeared before them, having seemingly materialized from thin air. Smith had almost forgotten with what incredible speed the gnomes could move when necessary.

From a pocket in his garment Milo produced a frayed roll of leather and extended it.

"My thanks, Milo," said the king as he took the scrap and handed it to Smith. Milo grinned widely before speeding off. "I do not know whether ye can make any sense of this, but I invite thee to try."

Smith gingerly unrolled the scroll and used the heel of his hand to smooth it atop the uneven surface of the rock. About ten inches square, the chart appeared to be of vellum; various ostensible landmarks, Roman letters, and runic characters were burned into it. Smith turned the map first this way, then the other, in an effort to orient it. Nothing on its timeworn surface looked familiar.

"What do these mean?" he asked, stymied, indicating symbols arranged randomly along the edges of the map.

Gob smiled ruefully. "I, myself, do not understand them," he apologized.

The ancient map was roughly divided into three sections by curved lines running through it. Burned into the chart near the top were saw-toothed images resembling small crowns. These Smith assumed to represent hills or mountains. His surmise was confirmed when he bent closer to the map in order to study it more carefully.

Faintly superimposed across one of the groups of serrated figures were the vague remnants of the letters NUS and, separately, N. Clearly, the Nustazien Highlands.

Smith looked up. "Is there a large stream or river nearby?" He recalled the glint of sunlight off a distant river upon emerging from the alchemist's lair.

The king pointed upstream from the small brook that purled at the base of the boulder upon which they sat. "This is but a tributary of the River Omer, located but one atru away, through the forest."

"How large is that river?"

"Quite large, indeed. In some places it is impossible to see from one bank of the Omer to the other."

"Where are its headwaters?"

Gob looked quizzical. "I do not understand. Although the Omer traverses our land, no one may vouchsafe its origin. The only certainty is that, some distance from here, the river becomes two. Where its waters ultimately lead is unknown."

Using a fingertip, Smith traced the course of the Omer. As indicated by the bygone cartographers, the river appeared to originate in promontories an unknown distance beyond the more moderate Highlands. Although two branches of the Omer were reflected toward the bottom of the map, Smith was unable to ascertain where, relative to the gnome's subterranean city, the division actually occurred because the map was evidently not to scale. Nor was he able to determine where either fork ultimately terminated.

"If these marks represent the Nustazien Highlands, how far from where we're sitting does the river divide?" he asked, pointing to the corresponding area on the map.

The king picked up the chart and held it near his face. After studying it a moment, he laid it aside and stood. Thoughtfully stroking his beard, Gob surveyed the surrounding landscape in silence.

"There, I think," he finally said, pointing. "No more than two atru in that direction.

Smith nodded wordlessly and resumed scrutinizing the document. One fork of the Omer appeared to pass between a series of hills before encountering a lacuna depicted along the left side of the map. A broad delta, where the river fanned out, was clearly delineated. Near the center of the chart, below the Nustazien Highlands, the river encompassed a wooded area before disemboguing into this apparent sea. Smith deduced this indicated the valley where the gnomes lived and where they were presently sitting. That the ancient mapmakers accorded the area especial significance was manifest by the care with which they memorialized it on the ancient scroll.

Enigmatic hieroglyphics suggested a scattering of landmarks or centers of population. The absence of scale, however, rendered it impossible for Smith to get any sense of the distances involved. He pointed to one of them.

"Do you know what this is? Have any of your people ever been here?"

King Gob shoot his head. "My people have not ventured beyond the confines of our valley within collective memory. And this map has lain undisturbed and unused for generations."

According to Lasceaux, traders from Kaelops regularly supplied him with materials necessary for his alchemical experiments. It was, ostensibly, the interruption of those supplies that prompted the alchemist to abduct Smith in the first place. Perhaps the Kaelops was one of the localities reflected on the chart. The fact that its citizenry engaged in trade, even with the loathsome alchemist, bespoke a relatively sophisticated culture that would perhaps prove sympathetic to his plight. Kaelops' inhabitants might even be able to provide information that would help Smith return home. A journey thither seemed, therefore, the most compelling course of action to pursue. He laid the map aside to solicit King Gob's advice.

After listening attentively, Gob soberly nodded. "When dost thou wish to depart?"

"As soon as possible. There is nothing to be gained by waiting."

"Truly, though I am greatly saddened to see thee leave us."

"I share your sorrow, King Gob. I will see you again, though, I am sure." Smith leaned over and fiercely embraced his diminutive friend.

VIII

An hour later found Smith tramping through the dense forest toward the River Omer with Milo as his guide. Over his back was flung a duffle bag containing fruits and nuts for his journey, a skin of water, a clean pair of trousers that Robert's wife had previously woven for him from flax, and another pair of the durable buskins that the elementals prized so highly. A tarnished astrolabe also nestled in his bag, a vestige of the gnomes' peripatetic ancestors and a superannuated counterpart to the vellum map that King Gob also insisted Smith take. Buried far down in the bag was the magnificent jewel that King Gob had presented to him upon their first meeting. Wrapped around Smith's waist was a thin blanket.

"We are almost there," called Milo over his shoulder. "Are ye certain that ye will not forestall your departure until a little later? Ye need not fear the alchemist while ye remain with us, I assure thee."

Smith tried to sound self-assured, even jovial, as he replied, "No, Milo, I'm afraid that I must leave in order to find my way back to my rightful place. I will see you again before too long, though, I am certain." The mere sound of these words, bravely spoken, help bolster Smith's sagging confidence. Milo, Smith noted uneasily, failed to echoed his forced enthusiasm.

The gnome abruptly stopped. "Ye can hear the Omer now," he announced.

Smith halted a few steps behind him and listened; the surging rush of a powerful river was discernable to his ears.

"It is just beyond those trees."

They advanced through the forest and presently found themselves standing on the bank of the River Omer.

The watercourse that swirled before them was approximately 50 yards wide. Near them, a small wooden boat bumped against a makeshift pier that extended into the current.

Milo turned toward Smith. "I now surrender thee to the embrace of Mother Omer, though I would fain ye abandon thy determination to leave and, instead, return home with me. Since I know this to be impossible, however, I bid thee a tranquil and productive sojourn and trust that ye will find a path back to us."

"I thank you with all my heart, Milo," said Smith, "and will never forget your many kindnesses. Friends like you are too rare to ever forget." The two stepped onto the pier where Smith leaned down and carefully deposited his effects into the little boat. He then squatted before his friend. "I hope to see you again before very long," he said. "Please extend my heartfelt gratitude to King Gob and Bolander and everyone else for me." He embraced the little man, his sorrow at parting being but ill-concealed.

Milo helped Smith clamber into the unstable boat. As soon as Smith was seated, Milo freed the rope which secured it to the jetty.

Smith used the wooden paddle that lay along the bottom of the craft to guide it into the center of the river. As the boat caught the Omer's current, Smith turned to look back toward the gnome still standing forlornly on the jetty.

"Goodbye, my dear friend!" Smith cried, even then fleetingly considering steering back to the bank of the river to rejoin his friends and the safety of their company. He reluctantly dismissed the idea...to remain with the elementals would necessitate that he live in continual fear of Lasceaux, whose physical propinquity to the gnome city would actually facilitate the alchemist's retribution. Worse, it would also subject his benefactors to the alchemist's vengeance. Ultimately, Smith realized that to reside indefinitely with the dryads was inconsistent with his desire to return home.

Directing his boat toward the heart of the river, Smith turned again and saw Milo slowly trudge toward the dark woods bordering the Omer, heading homeward. The gnome's final entreaty floated across the water.

"Farewell, Smith. I wish thee life, prosperity, and health."

***

Based on the position of the sun, Smith estimated that two hours of daylight remained. He'd been on the river about three hours, he guessed, and had not seen any other creatures except a few birds that skimmed along its surface, the tips of their slender wings scattering water droplets like shimmering diamonds. The woodland that lined the Omer was unbroken by glades or fields, the river's course unimpeded by shallows or obstructions.

Smith retrieved his map and quickly scanned it. By noting the movement of the shadows along the channel as he slipped along, and assuming the sun traveled from east to west, he determined that the Omer flowed generally south and west. Smith hadn't the slightest idea how distant any of the locations shown on the map actually were nor, because of its antiquity, could he rely on the chart's inherent accuracy. Though it suggested that the Omer eventually debouched into a sea, he could not be certain whether that was still the case or, indeed, whether such a sea ever existed.

He replaced the map in his duffle and drank deeply from the bota. The sun warmed the top of his unprotected head and its reflection upon the water flashed into his eyes like a lance. The only sounds that reached Smith's ears were the murmurings of the river and the sigh of the breeze that gently rustled the dense vegetation crowding its banks. The Omer's flow was gentle and devoid of serpentine convolutions, rendering it unnecessary for Smith to dip his paddle into the river to prevent the tiny craft from drifting too far toward either bank.

***

For the remainder of the day Smith guided his boat down the placid Omer. When the sun finally began to droop languidly below the treetops, he steered his craft onto the farther bank of the river and dragged it out of the water to preclude the possibility of its being carried away by the current during the night. Because he lacked a proper bedroll, he scoured the area nearby until he located a plot of luxuriant grass. Smith avidly picked a generous armload and carried it back to the riverbank, where he deposited it beneath the sheltering boughs of a tree. Returning to gather more, he soon created a plush cushion admirably suited for sleeping, atop which he placed his blanket. Smith was confident the clement temperatures would render additional shelter unnecessary.

As quickly as the sun descended a canopy of stars began to glimmer in the empyrean, though Smith was able to identify no familiar constellations. He eased himself onto his makeshift bed and leaned wearily against the tree that served as a headboard. The breeze of the early afternoon had subsided and the soothing ebb of the Omer seemed in harmony with Smith's rhythmic breathing. He closed his eyes as he meditatively chewed some nuts from his knapsack.

In moments he was asleep.

For two additional days Smith navigated the Omer in his small craft, resting each night along its mossy bank. The nights were temperate and lent themselves to comfortable and invigorating repose. Notwithstanding that he carefully rationed his dwindling cache of food, Smith's anxiety over its depletion was immeasurably assuaged when, on the third day, he chanced to discover a pear tree growing near the river, its branches resplendent with fruit.

That same evening, Smith beached his boat preparatory to making camp on the river's shore. During the course of his subsequent exploration of the riverbank for suitable bedding material, he was simultaneously excited and apprehensive to discover that large sections of land had been denuded of trees. Someone had indisputably cleared the area long ago; examination of the stumps revealed their top surfaces to be encrusted with a thick coating of hardened yellowish resin. Because no logs were anywhere to be seen, it seemed likely that whomever had hewn the trees had thereafter floated them downriver, for Smith had encountered no roads upon which such a quantity of timber could be readily transported.

The clearing of forests invariably betokens the presence of organized settlements, where the lumber is used in the construction of habitations. Smith surmised this to be as true here as in his own world and concluded that a population center must therefore exist somewhere farther downriver. Of its size or distance he could not conjecture.

Smith rapidly collected material with which to cushion his bed and returned to his campsite at the river's edge. He would not rest as comfortably tonight as previously because of the paucity of cushioning material: only some prickly twigs of oak and dry grass. He placed his blanket, duffle bag, and spare trousers atop this incommodious mat and, lying down, reflected on a plan for returning to his world. The imminent prospect of encountering a settlement crystalized the need for a definite strategy.

After several minutes of quiet reflection, Smith concluded the most sensible thing to do upon reaching whatever town lay ahead would be to seek out a prominent resident who possessed knowledge sufficient to advise him. Surely not every inhabitant of this world was a votary of the loathsome alchemist. And, given his present, parlous circumstances, Smith realized that he had painfully few alternatives.

He retrieved a pear from among his supplies. The jewel that King Gob gave him glittered among his few possessions and Smith knew that its value as an exchange medium might soon become necessary.

Smith wearily sighed. There was still at least a half-hour of daylight remaining. His hand strayed to the beard which had lately enveloped his face. He must, he thought, present a very rough image after so many days of inattention to his appearance. He slowly chewed the pear and gazed idly into the evening sky overhead. A large bird glided across his field of vision and vanished from view beyond a clump of brush. He lay still a moment, thinking, then bolted upright in consternation. The grey plumage of the bird was unmistakable. It was an Ansut!

Smith leaped to his feet, uncertain as to what the appearance of the creature augured. Perhaps it was only a wild Ansut, one untamed by the alchemist. Gob had informed him that the alchemist trapped them from their wild state, after which he trained them to serve him. If this was so, there was no cause for alarm. But what if the bird was, indeed, an emissary from Lasceaux? Smith knew that his location, and vulnerability, would then be revealed to his nemesis.

For good or ill, Smith's dilemma was resolved a moment later when the Ansut emerged from the straggly vegetation behind which it had previously disappeared. It awkwardly hopped toward Smith flapping its powerful wings, stirring up bits of dry leaves and twigs. Smith was uncertain how to react as the bird folded its glossy wings against its sides and tucked its scaly arms to its breast. The creature cocked its head to one side and, to Smith's astonishment, began to speak in a hoarse, rasping tone.

"Monsieur Lasceaux conveys his compliments and assures you that he will render it possible for you to return from whence you came, as your services in this world are no longer necessary."

Fortunately, Smith was quickly able recover his poise. "Tell him that I decline his assistance and intend to return without his aid."

The bird eyed Smith balefully. "Monsieur Lasceaux is wise to your intentions. I have been observing you since you departed the fatuous dwarfs and have regularly apprised my master of your progress, if it can be characterized as such. Even now he follows close behind, but bade me inform you of his magnanimous offer. Should, through some quirk, you reach the hamlet that lies ahead, you are acquainted with no one who resides there and will fare very badly. You cannot survive much longer in this world. Be wise. Hearken to the generosity of Monsieur Lasceaux and wait here for him, as he will shortly arrive."

The Ansut's revelation confirmed what Smith had already deduced: the existence of a town downstream.

"Why should Lasceaux suddenly concern himself with my welfare?" he asked.

"My master has had much time for reflection since your departure. He realizes it was error to abduct you, has repented of his misjudgment, and now wishes to make amends for his earlier lack of hospitality."

The alchemist obviously hoped, by his artless ploy, to induce Smith to promptly surrender, thus sparing Lasceaux the inconvenience of having to pursue him. Smith entertained no doubt that if he were once again reduced to captivity, he would suffer poignantly.

"I have no intention of surrendering to Lasceaux."

"You would be well advised to temper your foolish bravado with prudence," advised the Ansut. "Monsieur Lasceaux does not readily suffer effrontery. I caution you not spurn his magnanimity."

"Perhaps I failed to couch my answer clearly enough. Here, then, is my response to Lasceaux's proposition." With this, Smith directed a robust kick at the feathered courier.

Startled, the Ansut awkwardly hopped backward, fluttering its wings to maintain balance. Malignant rage filled the bird's eyes when it righted itself. Saying no more, the myrmidon extended its scrawny arms and sprang upward on outstretched wings. It wheeled in an ascending spiral until it was lost overhead in the darkening sky.

Smith was unnerved by the appearance of the alchemist's emissary and made rapid preparations to abandon his campsite. If the declarations of the Ansut were true, Lasceaux was probably only a relatively short distance away. Furthermore, Smith's passage along the Omer was sure to be continuously observed by the Ansut, who would report his whereabouts to the pursuing alchemist.

The settlement that lay upriver might afford him a degree of protection if he succeeded in blending with its population, though of their nature or appearance Smith knew naught. Despite this lacuna, it was essential that he reach the community without delay, before Lasceaux caught up with him.

Smith hastily tossed his meager belongings into the small craft and shoved it into the river. It was now too dark to identify distinct objects on the opposite bank except for the gaunt saplings that punctuated the shore. Fortunately, the moon in its first quarter cast sufficient light to enable him to safely navigate his boat along the tranquil river. Periodically, a small aquatic creature would break the surface of the waterway and the resulting splash would startle Smith. Otherwise, the only sounds were the soft ripple of his oar as he periodically dipped it into the Omer and the reassuring music of the undulating river itself. Its dark banks were quiet, and neither the icy moon nor the gleam of ancient stars spangling the heavens disclosed any movement among the brooding vegetation.

Smith plied the ebon waters of the Omer all night, intermittently using his oar to guide his boat, the celestial orbs his only companions. As the hours of the night dragged past, the stars, one by one, group by group, began to dissolve into the quickening sky, presaging the dawn. Smith was fatigued from his nocturnal voyage, as he had not slept for a day and a night.

At once, his faculties were arrested by the thin smell of wood smoke drifting through the cool, damp air. He was nearing the settlement spoken of by the Ansut. Smith instinctively glanced upward at the thought of the evil creature but saw no evidence of the spy.

Smith's pulse quickened as he drifted toward the cryptic outpost. He quickly collected his belongings in the bottom of the boat and began paddling in order to augment the Omer's gentle current. The sun was already creeping above the treetops, revealing a pale stratum of smoke suspended in the morning air. Gnats and midges swarmed thickly about Smith's unprotected head but he paid them little heed as the scent and density of the smoke increased with each stroke of his oar. Where he would go upon entering the settlement he knew not...he knew only that he must seek asylum from the relentless alchemist.

IX

Smith encountered the first habitation before even realizing it.

Emerging from the hazy morning air in the middle of a rough clearing on the left bank of the river was an unprepossessing shanty, a wisp of smoke rising lazily from its crumbling chimney. Though apparently occupied, Smith was unable to detect any active signs of life around the cottage. As he slowly drifted past it, however, he caught sight of a plump figure tending a small garden. Garbed in tattered clothing, the individual appeared oblivious to Smith's presence. The figure's hair was pulled tight and knotted at the back, revealing a wrinkled but unremarkable, seemingly female, profile. Smith saw no other persons about, but elected not to greet the villager. He resumed paddling, leaving the diligent gardener behind.

Minutes later Smith arrived at a second cottage abutting the river, but its forlorn appearance and overgrown yard bespoke its abandonment. Increasingly, the air smelled strongly of smoke.

Minutes later Smith arrived at a second cottage abutting the river, but its forlorn appearance and overgrown yard bespoke its abandonment.

As he glided past the lifeless house, a distinctly human voice floated across the river. Although Smith could not discern specific words, its human timbre was unmistakable and he was taken aback by its unexpectedness.

Additional structures began to loom from the verdure, each emitting pungent wood smoke from stone chimneys. All appeared to be constructed of hewn wood in varying degrees of decay, chinked with mud, and had high, sharply peaked roofs. Bereft of conventional windows, the dwellings possessed only wooden shutters flung open against their collapsing walls, exposing gaping, windowless voids. In the yards of several, Smith saw beings in trousers or crude smocks chopping wood, weeding small plots, or repairing a broken gate or shutter. A few individuals slumped in doorways and gazed at him sourly as he floated past, though none hailed him.

By and by, a broadening in the river disclosed a mélange of houses, cottages, and huts, all crowded together along the banks of the Omer for as far as Smith could see. Several rickety wharves thrust into the river at various points along its length, to which were haphazardly moored a collection of deteriorating rowboats and flimsy rafts. Narrow dirt lanes led from these quays into the warren of weathered buildings that comprised the town. Odiferous clouds of wood smoke rose from many chimneys as its inhabitants strove to ward off the chill of the morning and the pungent odor of fish hung heavily in the air. The entire tableau fairly reeked of a commingling of the two odors. Slouching along the thoroughfare nearest the river, Smith beheld exemplars of the citizenry, all of whom were clad in the crudest of attire. Disjointed fragments of conversations drifted across the water as Smith anxiously guided his craft toward the nearest dock.

Smith's boat bumped gently into the mooring post of the quay. He gingerly climbed from the craft and lashed it to the pier. Although a few individuals passively noted his arrival, no one accosted him. Carefully securing his jewel and map in the folds of his clothing, Smith left the balance of his possessions in his knapsack in the bottom of the boat and walked briskly down the wooden dock to the connecting street where he approached the first individual he encountered.

"Good morning, friend," Smith saluted the man.

The rustic was scarcely five feet tall and sported a tangled brown beard and thick, bushy eyebrows. Smith judged him to be approximately 30 years old.

Rather than acknowledge the salutation, the man simply strode ahead without establishing eye contact. Perplexed, Smith walked on, utterly ignorant of local customs but anxious not to offend the inhabitants.

Smith arbitrarily chose a narrow dirt lane branching off the main thoroughfare and followed its meandering course among decaying cottages with sagging walls. Bare patches on their steep roofs were once covered with wooden shingles that had long ago broken free and tumbled to the ground, where they now lay in moldering heaps. The shutters of all the habitations were tightly closed and billows of white smoke spewed from a forest of chimneys and stovepipes.

Smith was as repulsed by the unkempt appearance of the town as by the surly attitude exhibited by its denizens but, lacking an alternative, continued on his way *in omnia paratus*. In not much time he saw another individual trudging listlessly toward him.

"Good morning, friend. I trust the day finds you well," Smith smiled, hoping to elicit even a token response.

The bumpkin drew up and suspiciously scrutinized him. "I am ill. Leave me alone," he churlishly responded.

"I intended no offense, friend. Forgive me as I am new to your village. Is there an inn here where I may obtain viands and lodging?" Although Smith had not the means of paying for such services, save with his priceless jewel, he felt it a reasonable inquiry and one that would assuage any suspicions the man might harbor about him. In point of fact, though, he was utterly exhausted.

A look of confusion darkened the man's face. "Nothing like that exists in Asem."

"The name of this village is 'Asem'?"

"Aye," the man grunted. "What business have you here?"

"My business is with your chief magistrate," Smith authoritatively lied. "Since there is apparently no inn hereabouts, please inform me where he may be found. It is important that I speak with your magistrate immediately, even before I secure lodging." Smith's tenuous position forced him to be more disingenuous than he would have wished.

"If you desire an audience with he who wields power, then you seek Ambilnar Dokai, satrap of Asem. Though your reasons are your own, you clearly hail from afar."

"I do, indeed, come from afar," Smith acknowledged.

"Your eagerness to meet with the satrap is ample proof of that," the man snorted. He glanced furtively about.

Smith thought a satrapy a peculiar office in such an Occidentalized settlement. "Where may your satrap be found?" he probed.

A sprinkling of Asem's uncouth citizens had silently materialized, peeping along the edges of houses or staring dumbly from open windows. The denizen pointed in the direction of a wooded hill.

"Dokai resides yonder, at the end of this road. If you continue along it without deviation, you will surely find him." With that, the man turned abruptly and hastened away without a rearward glance.

Smith surveyed the grim visages of the inhabitants who had been monitoring their conversation: men in shapeless overalls, soiled shirts, and clumsy brogans; women in coarse frocks and bare of foot, the hair of both sexes growing in wild disarray. He forced an uneasy smile at the stoic faces and began trudging up the muddy lane toward the apparent home of Asem's burgomaster.

He hadn't the slightest idea what he was going to say or do once he arrived there.

X

The home of Ambilnar Dokai formed an outlandish contrast to the decrepit structures that otherwise characterized Asem. Situated in the purlieus, enveloped by dark woodland unmolested by the woodsman's axe, the garish edifice was constructed of cyclopean blocks of marble. Arabesque pilasters of veined rose quartz supported an entablature that extended the length of the building, from which jutted the heavy wooden beams of the veranda, as black from creosote as from age. The other end of the great beams rested on sculpted columns of the same rose quartz. Appearing to be at least three stories, the topmost floor boasted ornate stained-glass windows, above which rose a steeply turreted roof sheathed in lead. Smith was unable to ascertain the gross dimensions of the house because dense trees crowded along the entire length of its exterior walls. Dokai's pretentious residence created a bizarre counterpoise to the hovels that comprised Asem's remaining structures.

From the elevated ground upon which Dokai's inharmonious residence stood, Smith was able to survey the entire village spread along the riverbank below. From that remove, Asem's squalidness was somewhat palliated and it even assumed a rather quaint aspect. Moreover, the miasma of decaying fish that permeated the town was whisked away by the breeze. The placid Omer bisected the town, which clung to its muddy banks for a distance of over a mile. Far downriver, Smith could vaguely discern where the Omer began to widen before disappearing into the mist.

Smith could see little evidence of purposeful activity on Asem's sodden lanes, although here and there an individual listlessly wandered about or tended one of its ubiquitous gardens. His attention was, however, immediately diverted to one of the rickety piers that jutted into the river.

A cowled individual had just stepped onto the quay from a small sailing craft, which he was in the process of securing against the gentle tug of the river. It was, in fact, the same pier where Smith's boat was tied as, even from afar, he could see it rocking in the mild current. Though the distance rendered it impossible to distinguish the traveler's facial features, Smith could easily tell that the figure was clad in a long, dark robe.

The newcomer straightened from his labors and stepped across the pier to Smith's boat. He stood motionless for a few moments, scrutinizing the small craft. Then, to Smith's astonishment, the figure stooped and speedily loosed the boat's moorings. The boat promptly began to drift away from the pier, toward the center of the river.

"Lasceaux!" spat Smith. The Ansut had spoken rightly. The vengeful alchemist was truly on his very heels. No doubt directed by his feathered agent to the location of Smith's craft, Lasceaux had quickly undertaken to prevent a waterborne escape by his quarry.

Smith turned and strode up the path that led from the end of the road to the Satrap's home. The thread of white smoke that rose from two flagstone chimneys at each end of its leaded roof attested to its occupancy. Striding onto the expansive stone veranda, he approached the only portal in sight. Of heavy carved wood, the massive door had affixed to it an elegant, if incongruous, knocker. Smith grasped it and, hesitating only a moment, announced his arrival with four solid raps. He stepped back two paces, straightened his back, and ran a sunburned hand through his bedraggled hair.

No one responded.

After a wait that seemed interminable, but which probably encompassed only seconds, Smith again stepped to the door and repeated his action. Still there was no answer, nor could he discern any sound beyond the great door.

As vexed as he was anxious, Smith knocked at the door a third time with appreciably more vigor. Presently, he heard the scrape of a bolt slowly being drawn from within and the door was leisurely opened to reveal a liveried individual standing at the threshold.

"My Lord has not summoned you. Depart immediately before I have you whipped back to Asem!"

The being who barked the hostile greeting was manifestly of the same genotype as the settlement's other uncouth inhabitants, but attired entirely in white and well groomed, with neatly trimmed beard and coiffured hair. He looked smugly at Smith.

"Salutations, sir. If this is the residence of Ambilnar Dokai I respectfully request an audience," Smith announced as formally as possible.

"You are a knave. Return to your place!" clipped the other man.

Though apprehensive about the reception he was likely to receive from the satrap, Smith was unprepared for such overt aggression from an obvious hireling. Repressing his anger, he responded, "I am a stranger to Asem and ignorant of your protocols. Forgive any offense in my manner, but I must repeat my request to see Ambilnar Dokai immediately."

"Master Dokai does not entertain his vassals. You assuredly know this. Return to your hovel while you are still able," stated the man, coldly.

The confrontational steward obviously had no intention of granting Smith entry. His intransigence notwithstanding, the alchemist was undoubtedly en route at that very moment. Smith possessed neither the leisure nor the inclination to argue with the obstreperous domestic.

"Be warned that I bear extraordinary news from His Majesty King Geronimo the Sublime, the particulars of which I am not at liberty to disclose to a mere servant," sniffed Smith. "Your master's appalling lack of hospitality ill befits a satrap of his renown. However, it is *you* who will answer to your master for your failure to heed me. Good day". Smith turned smartly on his heel and began striding away, silently praying that his ruse would be successful.

As he stepped from the veranda, he heard, "Halt!"

Smith smiled inwardly and continued walking.

"Stop!" The servant exited the building and hastened after Smith. "Wait, wait. I will inform the satrap," he called. Smith stopped and slowly turned to face him.

"I will undertake one circuit of this structure," Smith warned, indicating Dokai's home. "If, by the time I return to this spot," he pointed to the ground at his feet, "you continue to obstruct me, I will take my leave. But make no mistake: it is *you* whom your master will hold accountable for my departure." Smith folded his arms and looked expectantly at the functionary.

"I will return presently."

As the man sped back into the house Smith ambled toward a corner of the edifice. Once the heavy door closed, Smith suspended his perambulation and simply waited where he stood.

The factotum returned in less than two minutes.

"I beg your forgiveness," he apologized. "I stupidly mistook you for a citizen of Asem. Please accompany me." He stepped aside to allow Smith to enter the edifice. "Master Dokai will, of course, grant an audience to the representative of the esteemed King Geronimo."

"Most wise," gravely asserted Smith.

The room into which he was admitted was an antechamber with several dark, carved doors opening from it. The floor was of polished wood and reflected a myriad of tiny flames that leaped and danced from candles in a golden chandelier suspended from the beamed ceiling.

The servant securely bolted the entrance then turned to their right, where he rapped twice on a wooden door girded with iron straps. Although Smith heard no sounds beyond it, the man grasped the handle and drew open the door. With a sweep of his arm, he ushered Smith into the adjoining room.

Smith hesitated a moment, then stepped boldly across the threshold. The attendant quietly shut the door behind him.

In a stone fireplace at the far end of the room a smoky flame struggled to remain alit. Near it stood a delicate figure clad in a dark djellaba.

"Greetings," the figure said in a wizened voice. "I am Ambilnar Dokai, Satrap of Asem. Whom do I have the honor of addressing?"

"I am Arthur Smith, Excellency. Thank you for granting me an audience."

"According to my timorous helot, it is I who should thank you for sparing me the cascade of miseries that would have befallen my humble residence had I declined. But, of course, he is a fool." Smith's host gestured toward a large ottoman in the center of the room. "Seat yourself."

Dokai padded noiselessly to a throne-like chair opposite Smith, gathered the folds of his embroidered djellaba about his spare frame, and eased himself down. Slippers of the same maroon brocade as his robe adorned his feet. The satrap's hair was full and white and his dark eyes shone like cinders from his waxen face. He clasped his pale hands in his lap, his nails long and yellow.

"Know that I am not deceived by your charade," Dokai calmly resumed in a thin, though not unpleasant, voice. "Though I am ignorant from whence you come, both your physical appearance and the trifling cleverness that you display readily establish that you are not one of Asem's insipid denizens".

Smith casually glanced about as he weighed an appropriate response.

The room was illuminated by heavy candelabra situated throughout. In the fireplace a log continued to burn feebly, although the room was, in fact, oppressively warm. Smith concluded that his host must be sweltering beneath his thick djellaba but, if uncomfortable, Dokai displayed no discomposure. Adjacent to the ottoman where Smith sat was a low wooden table, upon which rested a carafe and a set of wooden drinking cups. A carpet of intricate design covered the entire floor and the room was crowded with sundry articles of furniture: lofty étagères, a collection of tables and chests, and a polished desk of glistening ebony. The satrap remained silent while Smith surveyed the apartment and its rich furnishings.

Finally, Smith replied, "Your observations are most perceptive, Excellency, though it was only because of your doorman's obtuseness that I was forced to engage in a pretext in an effort to secure an audience with you. I trust you will forgive my innocent perfidy."

"As I informed you, my helot is a fool. So, too, the entire population of this region," the satrap added.

"It is true that I am not from this area. My home lies beyond the River Omer. Recent circumstances render it necessary that I travel to Kaelops, where I have important business. Given your position as satrap of Asem, I am hopeful that you will be able to provide assistance to that end."

"I am acquainted with Kaelops," Dokai acknowledged, "though it is greatly distant. But it is a curious business that compels one to leave his homeland, travel to a foreign city, then beg the assistance of strangers while perpetrating intentional deceptions upon them." Although Dokai spoke softly, his tone was distinctly menacing.

Smith had hoped, perhaps naively, to find someone in Asem in whom he could confide without reservation. Although initially uncertain whether the satrap would prove to be that individual, a gnawing suspicion to the contrary began to manifest itself in the pit of Smith's stomach. Despite his misgivings, Lasceaux's abrupt appearance in Asem made decisive action, one way or another, imperative.

"Because I am a foreigner and a stranger to Asem, I am curious, Excellency, of the nature of your domains." Smith posed his inquiry with feigned interest. "It was one of the townspeople who kindly directed me to your residence."

The satrap paused before responding. "Because you are a guest in my home, albeit an uninvited one, hospitality compels me to satisfy your inquiry. This entire region," he extended his left arm and swept it about, suggesting an area of indeterminable extent, "lies within the realm Omnipotent Celestial Empire. I have the honor of having been appointed satrap of

Asem and its environs through the munificence of His Incomparable Majesty, Duhab-Valank Rek."

"Where is capital of your empire located?" Smith asked.

"The Imperial City rises at the confluence of the Greater and Lesser Rivers," replied Dokai, testily. "I find it difficult to believe, sir, that you are as unlearned as you pretend."

Smith ignored the satrap's reproach. "Can you tell me, Excellency, whether Kaelops is also a part of your redoubtable empire?"

The satrap viewed him coldly. "I remind you, sir, that you are a guest in this house. Your inquisition is beginning to vex me and I find your questions wearisome."

"I beg your forgiveness, Excellency. I ask these things only because I am a simple man, unaccustomed to the ways of the world outside my humble village," Smith hastily backtracked. "If you will but grant me a moment longer, I will gladly take my leave and trouble you no further."

The satrap leaned back against the cushions and eyed Smith critically. "By what means do you propose a sojourn to Kaelops?"

"My hope is to engage someone to convey me there. Do you consider that feasible?" Smith asked with calculated diffidence.

"Perhaps," replied Dokai, cagily. "Though Kaelops is located far from here, on the shore of the Great Sea, and is unfrequented. A voyage there would be difficult and fraught with peril. Fortunately, I am acquainted with individuals who might be willing to hazard such an enterprise, though it would prove dear. It is an arduous journey and not without considerable hazard, for the Great Sea teems with freebooters. And, if I may speak frankly, you do not appear to possess resources proportionate to the risks such a voyage would entail."

Smith hesitated, then grudgingly reached into his garment and produced the jewel given him by King Gob. His desperate situation afforded no other option.

"This is surely adequate to provide me with the means to reach Kaelops."

Dokai arched his eyebrows. He leaned forward and plucked the gem from Smith's hand. "Lovely," he cooed as it sparkled in the subdued light. "From whence did you get this?"

"It has been in my family for many generations," Smith lied. "Because of the pressing nature of my business I am reluctantly forced to employ it as a medium for barter."

The satrap returned the jewel to Smith, who secured it in his clothing. "I now understand why you travel in the guise of an indigent. Your mission to Kaelops must indeed be of the greatest urgency. You certainly would not undertake a mere trifling journey with such a valuable treasure on your person."

"You perceive my situation most admirably, Excellency. Are you disposed to assist one burdened with such profound responsibilities?"

"Most assuredly I am!" cried Dokai with unexpected passion. "Rest assured, sir, that I am convinced of your sincerity and good will, and shall do everything in my power to ensure the successful completion of your mission. At the threshold, I shall stand surety for you and personally arrange for your immediate departure for Kaelops, where you may attend to whatever matter beckons so implacably. Meantime, you shall be supplied with fresh garments as well as viands."

Smith was anxious to decamp before Lasceaux's inevitable arrival at the satrap's residence. Dokai stood and actually seemed to float to a corner of the room where a tasseled cord was suspended.

"I shall be away only briefly," the satrap assured him as he tugged the cord. Moments later the servant whom Smith had previously encountered opened the door and entered.

"Bring our guest victuals and strong coffee," he ordered. "Make certain he is well fortified, for I doubt that he has supped well since leaving his homeland and he has a difficult journey before him." The servant nodded crisply then turned and left the room, shutting the door behind him. Smith rose as the satrap glided toward the door.

He turned to Smith before exiting. "Our coffee is renowned for its flavor and I am confident that our cuisine will be to your liking. While I'm away please consider my home as your own. My absence will be a brief one." So saying, he quickly departed, leaving no opportunity for reply.

Smith tiredly sank back onto the ottoman. Within seconds the servant reappeared carrying a tray which he placed on the low table. He bowed silently and exited.

The tray contained only four items: a small plate of rice blanketed with viscous gravy, a steaming decanter of coffee, a stone drinking vessel, and a wooden spoon. Ravenous, Smith swiftly devoured the rice, which he found to possess a mild nut-like flavor, while the sauce was heavily spiced. He filled the cup with coffee and reclined into the cushions to savor it. A pleasant feeling of well-being began to steal over him.

He was eager depart both Asem and its distasteful satrap, leaving Lasceaux far behind in the process. Although Smith hadn't the slightest idea what he would find in Kaelops, or whether it would bring him nearer to his goal of returning home, his prospects appeared to be improving.

Smith finished his coffee, placed the empty cup on the tray, and settled deeper into the ottoman's cushions. Hopefully, Dokai would return sooner, rather than later. Until then, he would nap, he thought as he closed his eyes.

XI

Smith awoke with a start. His eyes flew spontaneously open to confront the monolithic blackness that enveloped him. Startled and confused, he forced himself to remain motionless until the chaotic thoughts that raced through his mind subsided. Only then did he endeavor to ascertain his whereabouts.

Although disoriented, Smith believed himself to be lying supine upon a hard, flat surface. In the distance he heard muffled voices and the heavy tramping of feet; nearer, faint squeaks and rumbles. The immediate atmosphere vibrated under the shuddering groans and knocks of a vessel plying its way through calm seas. Indeed, Smith was distinctly aware of the sensation of movement as he felt himself rocking sluggishly to and fro.

He attempted to sit upright but found his torso encircled by fetters which prevented it. His legs were likewise bound but the darkness frustrated attempts to examine his restraints. Deep within him fear began to gnaw afresh.

Smith laid perfectly still and tried to recall where he was and how he had arrived there. Despite his efforts, he could remember nothing beyond his encounter with Ambilnar Dokai, and even that only vaguely. That he was at that moment a prisoner aboard some sort of ship seemed evident. By whose agency he'd become reduced to that status he didn't know, nor did he have the slightest inkling of the vessel's identity or destination. Under the circumstances, all he could hope is that he was bound for a place far from Lasceaux.

At some point during his deliberations, sleep must have stolen over Smith's over-burdened mind, for he was abruptly awakened by the tempestuous entrance of a huge, sinewed man clad in threadbare trousers and bare of chest.

"Wake up!" the giant roared as he directed a savage kick at the pallet that served as Smith's bed. Smith's head bounced painfully on the rough wooden surface and, had he not been fettered, he would assuredly have been thrown to the floor.

"Eat," growled the man as he placed a steaming bowl beside his prisoner and began to unlock the massive irons that restrained him. Smith groggily sat up and looked around at his surroundings, illuminated by the light that streamed through the open doorway that had lately admitted the intruder.

The fetid chamber where Smith found himself was low-ceilinged and cramped. Narrow planks were bolted along three of its walls. He occupied one and, to his surprise, on another an emaciated individual lay, more dead than alive. The man stared blankly into space, making neither movement nor sound. All of the planks were outfitted with shackles and leg irons. The small door in the fourth wall provided the only means of access to the room. Beyond it, leading upward, Smith could see a narrow flight of steps. The walls of his prison were of wood, as were the floor and ceiling. The bowl beside Smith contained a watery broth in which floated the decapitated heads of various fish. Their vacant stare unnerved him.

"Where am I?" he asked the jailer who slouched against the wall, massive, tattooed arms folded against his broad chest. The man looked quizzically at Smith for a moment, then snaked out a monstrous paw and cuffed him across the head.

"Nobody speaks here unless they're asked a question, mate." He laughed uproariously at the flush of anger that reddened Smith's face. "Now, either fill your belly or work hungry; it makes not a hair's difference to me."

Although ravenous, Smith was hesitant to avail himself of the ichthyic potage. Still, he tipped the receptacle to his lips and poured the foul liquid into his mouth. Though doing so caused him to wretch, he scooped the lifeless fish heads from the bottom of the dish and ate them, as well. The rapidity with which he ate, coupled with the repugnant nature of the meal itself, nauseated him.

"Better not lose it, mate. You'll not get another meal until tomorrow. The bowl is yours...lose it or suffer it stolen and you'll not get another," said his keeper, who had been watching Smith in bemused silence.

By employing a series of regular deep breaths, Smith managed to quell his rebellious stomach. His jailer straightened.

"Follow me," he ordered. He turned and ducked through the small doorway and began to ascend the stairs.

Smith eased himself to the floor and clutched the plank until he could steady himself against the perceptible movement beneath his feet.

A thought instantly exploded into his brain: his gemstone!

Smith's hand dove into the folds of his clothing where he had last placed the ruby. Gone! Gone, too, was his map! Frantically he patted himself all over, only to realize that he was no longer in possession of either article. Both had apparently been taken from him, undoubtedly by Dokai, after he had fallen asleep in the satrap's home.

Completely devastated, Smith wobbled to the door and began trudging up the steps, sick at heart. His cell mate moaned almost imperceptibly as he was once again abandoned to perpetual darkness.

As he surmised, Smith was aboard a ship. Several men were visible on deck, busily engaged in one activity or another. Here, a man repaired rigging; there, some others adjusted a staysail; elsewhere, seamen mopped the deck or set canvasses. Placed long the periphery of the deck at regular intervals was a ring of squat naval canons, their muzzles pointing through the railing toward the vacant expanse of sea that encompassed them. No flag hung from any mast or line; of the nature or registry of the vessel Smith was ignorant, although he suspected much. Smith's jailer handed him a pole, one end of which was swathed in rags, and a bucket of dark, greasy water.

"Get over there and start swabbing out the guns," he commanded. "Begin with those on the port and work starboard, bow to stern." The man pointed, indicating the order Smith was to follow...huge, twisted veins roped their way along his swarthy arm and spread across his pectorals; his anthracite beard fairly glistened in the sunlight. "Peter!" the giant bellowed at a slight man securing an errant clew line, "get over here!" The man quickly finished his task then ambled over. "Help him," the giant ordered, indicating Smith. "I have already given him instructions." So saying, he strode toward another group of men wresting a recalcitrant crossjack.

Smith looked at his assigned helper. "My name is Arthur. Do you speak English?"

"Aye, I speak English." Peter extended his hand, which Smith gladly shook.

The two men slowly picked their way across the bleached deck toward the canon. Because the muzzles of the guns projected through the ship's railing and overhung the water, it was necessary to slide their carriages backward on iron tracks screwed to the deck.

Smith laid his cleaning materials aside and grasped the ponderous gun. Looking expectantly at Peter he asked, "I guess the easiest way to clean these things is to pull them backwards in order to reach the muzzle, huh?"

His companion grabbed the opposite side and together they muscled the unwieldy gun rearward, where Peter locked it into place. Smith grasped his makeshift mop and, after soaking it in the bucket, began to vigorously swab the bore. Peter watched disinterestedly then asked, "You're from Asem?"

"No, from a place farther upriver."

"Does it have a name?"

Smith removed the mop from the muzzle of the canon and dunked it in the pail of water. "You wouldn't have heard of it," he smiled.

"Perhaps not, though I've long believed that other lands must exist along the upper regions of the Omer. Besides, your clothes are not of Asem." Dokai's promise to give Smith a fresh change of clothes was simply another deception.

"You're from Asem, then?" Smith asked.

"Aye, as are many others on this ship."

"What is this ship?"

"She is the Harpy, a corsair," Peter said, confirming Smith's suspicion.

"How did I get here? Do you know?"

"You were crimped, as was every other member of her crew, save the captain and Ling. In Asem and its environs, Ambilnar Dokai crimps for the Harpy. Elsewhere, different men do the same for other ships."

Smith finished dousing out the canon and, after drying the bore, he and Peter dragged it back into position and secured it in place before moving to the next gun.

"Is that the captain?" he asked Peter, nodding toward the bearded giant who obviously wielded great authority.

"That is Ling, the first-mate. The captain is in his cabin."

"Where are we bound?"

"Wherever the captain dictates. Wherever there is plunder. Wherever there is sanctuary." Peter hesitated. "It is always like this; the new ones are full of fears and questions. I, too, was like you. It was my hope that, if you were from Asem, you might know of my wife and children." The man stared wistfully across the featureless waters.

"I'm afraid I wasn't in Asem long enough to become acquainted with anyone." Smith speedily related the details of his meeting with Dokai, omitting much but mentioning that all his money, as well as his map, had disappeared.

"The food and drink that Dokai provided you was drugged. He stole your money before surrendering you to Ling. Ling loaded you into a dinghy, brought you aboard, and placed you in the brig until you recovered. You seem none the worse for it," Peter wryly smiled.

Too late Smith sadly realized that he should have heeded the advice of the satrap's doorkeeper and shunned any association with Dokai. "Any idea how long I was unconscious?" he asked Peter.

"You were carried aboard two days ago. How long you slept prior to that I do not know."

The two men continued their chore as they quietly conversed.

"Who is the man I saw in the brig with me?"

"He is called 'Shams.' He is sick with fever."

"Why is he locked up?"

"He is sick with fever." repeated Peter.

"Can't he be helped?"

Peter shrugged. "The Harpy has no infirmary, though there are three pallets in the brig. If a man is sick or insubordinate, he is chained to the first. If another is goaled for like reason, the first man is moved to the second pallet and the newcomer assumes his former place. This continues until all three pallets are occupied. If a fourth man thereafter proves disobedient or ill, the first man is cast overboard in order to make room for the new arrival. Thus, upon reaching the third pallet the bitter embrace of the sea will inevitably mend whatever malady led to the confinement of the first unlucky crewman. Until your arrival two days ago, Shams occupied the first pallet. His days among the living are therefore already numbered, contingent only upon the conduct and hardiness of the remaining crew."

"Won't Shams be restored to the first pallet now that I'm no longer occupying it?"

Peter shook his head. "You were placed below deck simply to enable you to recover from the drugging you suffered in Asem. Once Shams was transferred to a successive pallet to make room for you, his fate was sealed and is irreversible. The briny deep will cure unhappy Shams of all his ills soon enough."

The men suspended their conversation and busied themselves as Ling stomped past. Afterward, Smith asked, "So I am destined to serve on this ship indefinitely?"

Peter shrugged again. "For as long as you live, subject only to the whims of Ling or the captain. But death and disease necessitate that crewmen be continually replaced. In fact, you took the place of a crewman who was lost a fortnight ago when we commandeered a freighter from Kaelops. A useless exercise it was, too...all we got for our trouble was a load of timber and a quantity of stones and powders. Booty is divided equally among the Harpy's crew, but Ling simply burned that worthless rubbish along with the ship that carried it."

This revelation made Smith's heart leap, for the vessel referred to might have been the alchemist's supply ship!

"Do you know where the freighter was bound?"

"To Asem, where its cargo was consigned, save the chemicals and powders which were to be transported farther upriver to a place along the Omer. I do not know exactly where. At least that is what one of her crewmen told me before I relieved him of his head."

There could be no doubt. The ship intercepted by the Harpy some two weeks previously had been destined for Lasceaux.   It was the resulting interregnum in supplies that compelled the alchemist to abduct Smith in the first place and, in a painful irony, who now found himself imprisoned aboard the very ship directly responsible for all of his late misfortunes.

"What is this chatter!" thundered Ling. "I am certain that Shams will happily welcome company to his cell and I will surely provide it unless the talk ceases. The new one is ignorant, Peter, but you know better. Mark me, hold your tongues lest you lose them."

"He does not speak idly," murmured Peter tersely. The two men abandoned their conversation and devoted themselves to their work in silence.

XII

For an uneventful two weeks the Harpy plied the clement waters of the Great Sea. During the waking hours Smith labored in the galley or scrubbed the ship's deck with a stiff brush.   At night, utterly exhausted, he and his shipmates slept as best they could upon thin burlap mats tossed on the floor of the ship's stifling bilge.

Only Ling and the captain enjoyed cabins along the quarter deck, the latter an ancient and withered Moloch whose name was known to no one but about whom fearful things were furtively whispered concerning voyages he made as a young seaman aboard a phantom vessel to fantastic lands said to lie where the Great Sea pours forth into the sky. The Harpy's cadaverous master appeared only occasionally on deck, where he peered rapaciously through an ancient brass telescope, hoping to spot hapless barks or argosies gliding unaccompanied over the open water.

During his forays on deck, the captain typically consulted with Ling, speaking quietly to his factotum through a mouth filled with the decayed remnants of what had long ago been teeth. As he spoke, the captain would sometimes point seaward, sometimes gesture toward a particular seaman who was covertly watching their conclave, or rub a palsied hand over his cretaceous and sallow face, pied with age, after which he would return to his cabin after admonishing Ling to carry out whatever instructions he'd imparted during their colloquy.

Actual operation of the Harpy was, accordingly, the first-mate's responsibility, who fulfilled his duty with equal measures of efficiency and brutality. If, for example, it was a seaman's misfortune to be pointed out by the captain during one of the latter's sojourns on deck, the unfortunate was instantly cast into the brig to await his inevitable brackish plunge. Smith personally observed two occasions where Ling, for reasons known only to himself, slammed crewmen to the Harpy's deck and gouged an eye from each writhing victim with his bare fingers.

Though the Harpy's dissolute crew regarded Smith with suspicion, he found Peter to be a likable companion. In quiet talks he discovered that Peter had been a crewman aboard the corsair for five seasons. Before that, he had resided in Asem for as long as he could remember. Peter spoke longingly of his home and vigorously defended its citizens against Smith's criticisms, attributing their seeming hostility to the constant predations of the satrap, which left them dispirited and suspicious.

"Perhaps you will one day return to Asem," suggested Smith.

Peter looked at him lugubriously as he answered. "Nay, I am condemned to remain aboard the Harpy until she founders or I am killed, unless fate should deprive me of even those doubtful blessings."

Although Smith did not associate with any crew members except Peter, he soon became aware of an undercurrent of discontented murmurings among the men. What at first merely displeased, then enflamed them, were not the brutal conditions under which they served, but the fact that the captain had failed to guide them to any cargo vessels in over a month. Aside from the quotidian monotony of their shipboard existence, the marauders hungered for booty. Mindful of the crew's simmering anger, Ling took counsel with the wizened captain, who ordered the brigantine landward, to a port where a catalogue of merchant vessels could be had. Accordingly, sails were set and the Harpy skimmed across the Great Sea, the crew somewhat mollified, for they divined the captain's intentions.

***

The approach of land was presaged by the appearance of vast numbers of sea fowl, which hectored the ship as it skimmed along the polished surface of the Great Sea. Gulls, terns, and a multitude of species unfamiliar to Smith wheeled and screeched overhead, filling the sky with their ruction. The crew took great delight in trying to snare such birds as made bold to light on the deck, or in smiting them with whatever objects were at hand. Incongruous by its presence amid the swarm, Smith was dismayed to recognized a solitary Ansut, which floated above deck and carefully studied the men aboard.

When the slender, dark finger of land slowly appeared on the horizon, the crew, save the scant few necessary to guide the Harpy, was herded below deck into the mephitic bilge in order to thwart attempts at desertion. Until liberated when the Harpy was again in open water, they would share the company of sleek rats and bold roaches in complete darkness. Smith was among those confined, while Peter remained above deck to direct the ship landward.

The Harpy doggedly plowed toward its destination. At first a dark, ill-defined mass, the land inexorably began to exhibit variations in elevation and composition. Inevitably, the contours of a seaboard city emerged as the water beneath the raider's hull assumed a lighter hue.

The captain had been to Jmar countless times in the past and he smiled to himself as he stood on the fo'c'sle squinting through his battered telescope, encrusted with verdigris. He surveyed Jmar's hoary waterfront and labyrinthine alleys, its rotting wharves, and the hodgepodge of boats and ships that lay at anchor in her twin harbors.

At length, the Harpy slid into Jmar's sheltered breakwater, whereupon the sallow captain ordered Ling to drop anchor. After a huddled discussion with his first-mate, it was decided that Ling would remain aboard, while the captain took one of the Harpy's dinghies ashore to consult with certain individuals possessing knowledge of all merchant vessels as had recently left port.

Choosing a pair of reliable crew men as rowers, the captain descended the rope ladder dangling from the corsair's weathered hull and departed.

XIII

Eventide came to Jmar and, with it, the lambent flickering of candles behind the salt-encrusted windows of its houses or the tiny portholes of ships bobbing in its harbor. All was quiet but for an occasional muted voice floating across the oily water from a hatch momentarily opened, or the mournful baying of a dog deep within the town.

Presently, the slap of oars against water reached Ling's attentive ears and he strained his eyes into the dimness to catch sight of his returning captain. In a moment the small boat containing the Harpy's master emerged from the gloom. The rowboat rapidly drew alongside the Harpy and its occupants clambered up the swaying rope ladder.

"Loose the men," croaked the captain. "We must put to sea at once." His directive was rapidly carried out and the men, freed from their noisome prison, quickly weighed anchor and unfurled the Harpy's ghostly sails. The canvas sheets grew taut in the seaward breeze as the ship angled out of the harbor.

Gazing over the railing, Smith watched the diminutive galaxy of Jmar's glimmering lights recede into the darkness until they faded completely from view. Though saddened, he was oddly serene even when Ling directed a kick at him, cursing his idleness and commanding him to begin charging the canons with powder and ball.

***

Smith and Peter toiled through the seemingly interminable night, readying the Harpy's deck guns. While they worked, Peter whispered how he and the other seaman had ferried the captain to Jmar, where he'd commandeered a tumbrel and ordered them to transport him into the heart of city, to an inaccessible and squalid ghetto. Peter related how he and his companion pulled the heavy cart through Jmar's narrow cobblestoned streets until they lost all sense of time or direction. The height and jettying of the deteriorating structures crowding Jmar's thoroughfares rendered useless any attempt to navigate by use of the stars. Peter related how their legs, backs, and arms ached from the strain of maneuvering the handcart through the dizzying maze of unmarked lanes and alleys. Only rarely did they pass beneath a lighted window, calcified with accumulated salt and grime, shining forlornly in the darkness. At no point during their tortuous sojourn did they encounter another soul, but the wizened captain relentlessly urged them forward, directing them without hesitation through the tangled maze of streets

After a time, the exact length of which Peter couldn't determine, they drew to halt before a massive building of great antiquity. The age of the enormous structure was manifestly greater than even that of the ancient waterfront, though Peter was certain the edifice was far removed from the harbor itself, for they had walked a long, if convoluted, distance and the air lacked the dampness and peculiar scent characteristic of the sea.

Instructing the men to await his return, the captain alit and limped across the uneven street to the looming edifice. Looking neither left nor right, he disappeared beneath a vaulted doorway and melted inside.

The two mariners sat upon the ancient broken cobblestones to await his return, for they knew not whither to escape and, consequently, resigned themselves to a protracted and cheerless vigil.

At length, a door opened and a pale figure emerged from the forbidding structure. Peter and his companion immediately recognized their captain as he slithered back to the waiting tumbrel.

"Return to the Harpy," hissed the old man. "My operatives inform me that a schooner is even now en route to Jmar and that her holds are awash with cargo. With a favorable wind we shall easily locate and intercept her."

***

Through the waning hours of the night Smith and Peter labored over the Harpy's canons, preparing them for the martial action they would presumably soon witness. Morning found them exhausted, especially Peter, owing to his nocturnal sojourn to

Jmar, but their enervation instantly dissipated when the lookout howled excitedly from the crow's nest.

"Ship, ho! She's starboard, a schooner under full sail!" The lookout paused to look intently through a spy glass. "I cannot see her colors, though she flees us."

Every hand raced to starboard to scan the horizon. Smith looked, too, but was unable to discern anything even remotely resembling a ship on the limitless expanse of water.

He muttered his skepticism to Peter, who responded, "It is small wonder that you see nothing. Yours are the eyes of the land. You must possess the eyes of the sea to perceive things of the sea. The schooner is there," he continued, pointing to a spot on the illimitable ocean. Still, Smith could discern nothing.

Ling roughly shoved several men aside at the railing and studied the open sea. A broad smile illuminated his weathered face.

"She draws too much water," he murmured. All listened attentively, for Ling's experience in such matters was well known. "We shall have no trouble taking her, for she is pregnant with cargo and cannot elude us."

He turned on his heel and the company of pirates fell to either side with one accord to form a passage through their ranks.

"Man your stations!" Ling barked. Shouting rapid orders to the steersman, he strode to the captain's cabin and rapped once. A faint voice from within bade him enter and the first-mate ducked through the door and disappeared into its foul interior.

The Harpy's crew rushed to their assigned places on deck. Smith and Peter were assigned as cannoneers for the eight starboard guns and they double-checked their ordnance.

Ling and the captain emerged from the latter's cabin and made their way to the prow, where a heavy telescope rested on a tripod. The captain trained it on the horizon. Moments later, a hideous grin lacerated his countenance.

"She is the Orison," called the lookout, still gazing through his telescope. "Two medium guns appear to be extent of her armament."

"Make directly for her," directed the captain.

"It is even now being done," Ling responded.

At his post Smith could scarcely contain his nervous excitement. The expectation of an imminent clash caused the blood in his temples to throb and the fatigue that previously oppressed him had vanished. His entire body trembled as he strained his eyes along the horizon in hopes of spotting the Orison.

Peter stood impassively at Smith's side. On the corsair's port side, directly opposite them, their counterparts also manned eight guns, while two additional cannon were mounted on swiveling turrets at the stern. Everyone aboard was silent as they awaited the impending battle. The captain and Ling remained at the bow, the former's telescope still trained seaward.

The minutes passed with agonizing slowness but, inevitably, there appeared to Smith's searching gaze a tiny dark spot far out to sea. As the Harpy raced toward it through the celadon water it began to metamorphose into the form of a ship, with grand white sails and a polished deck that gleamed in the golden sunlight. Although they were still too far away for Smith to distinguish specific activity upon its deck, he could already see that their quarry rode low in the water and labored sluggishly despite the tautness of her canvas.

Ling stomped from the Harpy's prow to her stern.

"Steer nigh to her port. We'll rake her hull when we pass within range," he instructed the steersman.

The latter rotated the ornate ship's wheel slightly and the Harpy began cutting toward the port side of the Orison. She was now sufficiently close to enable Smith to discern several figures on her deck, all of whom were intently watching the Harpy's maneuvers. Uncertain of the newcomer's intentions, yet mindful of the potential danger to his vessel by exposing the Orison broadside, her captain rapidly altered her course, steering his ship starboard, and headed obliquely away toward the open ocean.

"Hard to starboard," commanded Ling. "She may flee but we shall overtake her, as the shark overtakes the cod. Hoist the colors, that she may know who hounds her!" One of the men clipped the ship's pennant to a line and ran it to the top of the main mast. Although the Orison was probably still too distant to recognize the flag, it bore the likeness of the eponymous monster from which the corsair took its name, superimposed upon an azure field.

The evasive action of the Orison initially afforded it a modest lead over the Harpy, but the swifter corsair inexorably began to narrow the distance between the two vessels. Finally comprehending the Harpy's hostile intent, the ponderous cargo ship attempted to lengthen its tenuous lead by sharply turning larboard, directly alee. Ling immediately recognized the folly of such an amateurish maneuver and simply ordered the Harpy 12 degrees to the larboard, certain they would swiftly overtake the Orison.

"Make ready to fire starboard guns!" he gleefully shouted.

In no more than fifteen minutes the Harpy had drawn abreast of the Orison at a distance of about 500 yards. Suddenly, a puff of white smoke blossomed from the schooner's deck; moments later a violent splash erupted in the water astern of the Harpy, accompanied by the boom of a cannon. An instant later the phenomenon was repeated, the projectile splashing many yards distant from the corsair.

"If it is a fight they desire, they shall not be disappointed. Only we shall wait until we are within range, for we will not be as prodigal with powder and ball as she," Ling cackled. He ordered the steersman to close the gap between the two parallel-running vessels.

Alarmed by the Harpy's encroachment, the Orison again directed cannon fire toward the advancing pirates, but Ling was undeterred.

"Upon my order cannonade the wretch!" he cried to the starboard gunners, Peter and Smith.

The gap between the two ships ineluctably narrowed. Though the Orison continually endeavored to outmaneuver its pursuer by sharply turning this way and that, it was to no avail...the Harpy bore down on her relentlessly. Even the incessant firing of the schooner's two ill-aimed deck guns proved ineffectual, for the projectiles were invariably short or wide of target, splashing harmlessly into the water.

Finally, Ling shouted, "Fire starboard guns!" Smith could see the Orison quite clearly now, for it was directly abreast of the Harpy at a distance of 150 yards. Its crew ran frantically about its deck, rapidly preparing for the close quarter fighting that was now only minutes away.

Peter took the torch that Smith held and applied its flaming tongue to the first of his cannons. The short fuse smoldered for a moment, then hissed loudly, emitting a thin stream of white smoke. An instant later the cannon exploded with a tempestuous roar, producing a cloud of acrid smoke and violently heaving itself rearward on the tracks affixed to the deck. The eyes of the entire crew were riveted on the Orison in anticipation of a direct hit.

An agonizing interval later, the Harpy's cannon ball ploughed into the sea in front of the freighter's bow. Peter automatically moved sternward, to the next of his eight cannons, and lit its fuse. Meanwhile, Smith began to swiftly reload the first gun.

The crack of the second cannon rent the air, only this time the eager pirates were rewarded by the sound of splintering wood as the ball struck the deck railing of the Orison, shattering a large section and killing two of its crew.

The eager pirates were rewarded by the sound of splintering wood as the ball struck the deck railing of the Orison.

The corsair's vile captain hooted loudly as he watched the mayhem through his prow telescope.

Because his ears still rang from the report of the cannon so close to him, Smith did not hear the explosion of the third cannon but looked up in time to see its missile crash through the hull of the Orison, high on her stern. A triumphant cry spontaneously erupted from the men aboard the Harpy while another cry, one of despair, simultaneously rose from the deck of the stricken vessel. A fourth cannon ball quickly followed, which struck the freighter amidships, slightly above her water line.

The merchantman defiantly launched yet another defensive cannonade against its aggressor, this time managing to strike the Harpy on its stern, well above the water line. Despite this, the entire ship convulsed under the impact and the artilleryman assigned to the swiveling stern guns was impaled by a spinning fragment of wood from the corsair's hull.

The Harpy having by now sailed beyond its reeling victim, Ling barked orders to turn hard about and approach it from the starboard. Gunners on the port side prepared to pound the luckless Orison. The corsair eased to within one hundred yards of the commercial vessel and was immediately met by a massive deluge of sea water from a cannonball falling only slightly short of its intended target.

"Commence firing!" shouted Ling. Like Smith and Peter previously, one cannoneer fired his guns, starting at the prow and moving sternward, as his assistant reloaded. As before, the guns exploded violently in clouds of smoke and flame. Three cannon balls ripped into the hull of the Orison in rapid succession, toppling her mainmast and causing water to flood into her bilge. Above the noise of the Orison's destruction the desperate cries of her doomed crew rent the air.

Because their proximity enabled them to place three direct, vital hits on their adversary, Ling elected not to waste the remaining port guns on the helpless ship. Instead, he ordered the Harpy to draw alongside as the crew prepared to board the Orison before she slipped beneath the waves. The ghoulish captain hurriedly retreated to his cabin, lest he be caught in the coming melee.

Smith was automatically handed a pike, though he scarcely took notice of it. The air crackled with excitement.

"What am I supposed to do with this?" he blurted to Peter.

"I suggest that you try to keep your head and body in mutual company," Peter stoically responded as he critically balanced in his hand the short cutlass given him and made practice thrusts and cuts in the air with it.

As the Harpy drew nigh the crippled freighter, several raiders began swinging over their heads in ever-widening circles heavy grappling hooks attached to ropes. When optimum velocity was reached, they released them toward the Orison, hoping to snag her. Some fell short and splashed into the sea or thudded harmlessly against her hull, but most of the grappling hooks landed solidly on the stricken vessel.

Every available hand aboard the Harpy immediately grabbed the thick ropes and, hand-over-hand, laboriously began to pull the two ships together. The crew of the ill-fated clipper responded with a panicked volley of shots from their muzzle-loading firearms.

"Be quick," urged Ling. "The fools must now reload." In truth, by unwisely discharging their flintlocks en masse, the men of the Orison had rendered it possible for the Harpy to approach virtually unimpeded.

Amid the jubilant shouts of her crew, the corsair nudged alongside the Orison

XIV

The crush of pirates balanced on the Harpy's railing sprang across the narrow crevice that separated the two vessels. Though two or three lost their footing and slipped between their grinding hulls, most gained the Orison's deck, where they were greeted by a thicket of poles and pikes wielded by the determined crew of the besieged freighter. Those in the vanguard fell immediately, their chests speared with wood or steel. Their companions swarmed over the bodies of their fallen comrades, indiscriminately slashing with their short sabers.

Ling drew his own pistol and, taking careful aim, shot a member of the Orison's crew in the throat. With a triumphant roar, the raiders surged forward as one, sweeping the wall of defenders before them. Smith, too, was swept up in the human inundation and quickly found himself aboard the hapless ship.

Here, a man hacked at another with a sword. There, two crewmen from the Orison desperately clubbed a pirate with maces. Nearby, another raider decapitated a man and, seizing his lifeless victim's pistol, turned and shot another in the back of his head. The cacophony of battle and the cries of the wounded filled the air. Smith stumbled over dead and dying but, because of the chaos swirling around him, was unable to locate Peter.

He suddenly turned and saw rushing toward him a crewman from the Orison, brandishing a cutlass. Instinctively, Smith leapt to one side to avoid his charge and, in so doing, realized that he still clutched the pike provided him aboard the Harpy.

Smith's attacker directed a fierce slice at him, which he was able to elude. He grasped his own weapon in both hands and cautiously thrust it toward the swordsman.

"I do not want to kill you," Smith muttered to himself, more to steady his nerves than to reassure his opponent, as the two adversaries warily circled one another. The Orison's crewman made a few mock lunges at him in an attempt to lure him out of his defensive posture, but Smith was not deceived by the feint. Instead, he continued to slowly circle the man, glancing quickly behind himself now and again to preclude an assault from that quarter.

Quickly wearying of the impasse, without warning the swordsman stepped toward Smith and raised his cutlass above his head, intending to bring it swiftly down and sever Smith's arm from his shoulder. Seizing the opportunity, Smith instantly drove his pike deep into the man's stomach. With an anguished wail, the swordsman toppled to the deck, a widening patch of blood staining his tunic.

Smith frantically pulled and twisted the shaft in an effort to dislodge the pike from the man's body. He finally succeeded and cast a swift glance around, spotting the corpse of yet another crewman from the Orison sprawled with a pistol grasped in its lifeless hand. Smith retrieved it but found the pistol to already have been discharged. Disappointed, he tossed it aside when a nearby tumult caused him to whirl in alarm.

Only a few yards away, Peter and a seaman from the freighter were engaged in a desperate *ballet de la mort*. The latter, who stood a head taller than Peter, was armed with a hand axe and small wooden shield. Peter still wielded his short cutlass. Using his shield to mask the disposition of the axe clutched in his other hand, the defender made a series of feigns toward Peter, then spontaneously swung his axe diagonally downward in an effort to cleave Peter's shoulder and neck. Peter leapt nimbly backward to avoid the blow and retaliated with rapid chopping blows with his sword, all of which landed harmlessly on the other's shield. The axe man stepped cautiously forward, still covering himself with his shield, forcing Peter to retreat a corresponding distance in order to maintain a defensible distance between them. Smith watched, mesmerized, the surreal drama.

Instantly, the seaman thrust his shield toward Peter's face with his left hand, while with his right he swung his axe viciously beneath it, at Peter's torso. Peter instinctively lashed out with his sword, striking the shield with a powerful chop that unintentionally embedded the blade deep into the wood. He simultaneously arched his body and the axe's curving trajectory missed him by a mere hair's breadth.

Peter, sans cutlass, scampered away just as his opponent launched another attack. Helpless, deprived of his weapon, Peter quickly glanced around for an avenue of escape. While his eyes were thus diverted, his assailant swung his shield in an arc, striking Peter a glancing blow along the side of his head and knocking him off his feet. In a flash, the axe man was astride his prostrate opponent, poised to deliver the killing blow.

Smith was instantly galvanized into action. Springing across the deck, he plunged his pike into the exposed side of the distracted seaman. The man spun around as the weapon's iron beak burrowed into his viscera. Peter quickly exploited his serendipitous reprieve by scrambling to safety.

The stricken crewman dropped his weapons and grasped his side with both hands in a futile effort to stop the flow of watery blood that spouted from the wound. Slowly, the man raised his head and looked with anguish directly into Smith's eyes. Saddened by the pain they held, Smith averted his gaze and stepped away.

The man weakly wrapped his fingers around the pike and gently pulled it free. Glistening sections of his entrails clung to its barbed head as it emerged from the hole in his body. Jerkily casting the pike aside, the man straightened, wobbled momentarily, then collapsed.

Peter approached Smith unsteadily. "I owe you my life," he panted. He smiled nervously and looked about the deck at the few struggles still in progress.

Most of the Orison's crew lay sprawled upon her deck in pools of blood. A few still battled heroically, but inexorably, one by one, they too succumbed to the relentless blows of the pirates. All sounds of violence finally ceased as the last man fell beneath the blade of Ling himself.

***

Smith and Peter picked their way among the fallen, searching for any signs of life, but the combatants had done their jobs with appalling efficiency. By their count, for each man killed from the Harpy, three had fallen from the Orison. The total number of dead from both crews totaled more than 25.

They were not accosted as they walked through the carnage.

Stillness descended over the Orison: the caesura of death. The sails of both vessels sagged listlessly and the tang of blood filled the torpid air.

With almost one accord, the victors began milling among the corpses, seeking to scavenge items from the bodies of their quondam owners. While Peter joined his shipmates in this grim diversion, Smith made his way toward a series of small cabins located on the quarter deck, where he encountered a number of pirates already engaged in systematically ransacking the compartments. Ling was nowhere in sight, presumably having repaired to the Orison's hold in order to determine the extent of the marauders' plunder.

One by one each locked cabin was breached and its contents brought to light. The first compartment had evidently served as the ship's armory, for wooden racks were built along its walls to accommodate the implements of war, while beneath them squat kegs of gunpowder were secured against the roiling sea. The arsenal was small and only perfunctorily equipped, bespeaking the mercantile character of the Orison.

The next cabin was likewise raided. Additional pirates, disappointed with the paucity of trinkets and jewelry found on the Orison's dead crewmen, had by now drifted over to join the spectators.

The second chamber clearly served as the captain's private quarters and contained the accoutrements of his vocation: log books, bills of lading, various documents and charts. The remaining diehards engaged in looting corpses now abandoned their fruitless enterprise and also made their way onto the crowded quarter deck. Ling and a handful of others remained below deck.

The door to the third cabin was also secured. Unlike the other two compartments, however, it stubbornly defied the pirates' initial attempts to breach it. The men redoubled their efforts by directing a number of heavy, well-placed kicks squarely on its latch. With a shudder, a shake, and a loud crack, the door finally yielded.

The man nearest the narrow doorway impulsively stepped across the threshold into the unlit cabin while his companions crowded forward. Because he had been among the first to arrive on the quarter deck, Smith enjoyed an excellent position from which to observe the incursion, though he struggled against the shoving and jostling of those around him.

A dull thud from within promptly sent the impetuous intruder stumbling backward. Blood gushed from a gruesome slash in his neck. Though he clamped his hand over the wound, blood spurted between his fingers and flowed down his arm. His eyes were already glassy, his pupils dilated with shock and fear.

The man's stunned companions rushed forward to aid their injured comrade, but for naught. His carotid artery and esophagus had both been severed.

With a terminal gurgle, the pirate fell to the deck, frothy blood boiling from the yawning wound.

In equal measure astonished and infuriated, the Harpy's bewildered crew hesitated to rush the cabin in order to deal with the assassins that obviously lurked within it. Someone secured a torch from the armory and used a flint and steel to ignite it, while another took a keg of gunpowder and, knocking a hole in it, rolled it into the lightless chamber, streaming explosive powder as it bumped along the Orison's deck. In a body, the remaining pirates retreated as flame was applied to the volatile trail, whereupon the torch was lobbed into the cabin.

The gunpowder instantly caught fire and burned rapidly, emitting a thick plume of pungent white smoke. The hissing flame raced through the doorway into the cabin's dark interior; the torch used to ignite it could be seen flickering on its floor.

Smoke from the scattered gunpowder filled the small unvented cabin. In seconds the flame would reach the powder keg. The men strained their eyes into the wall of thick smoke that filled the cabin, but could discern no movement from within. Even the torch burning upon the floor was but dimly visible through the acrid haze.

The pirates readied themselves to receive the charge of whomever was inside.

From the interior of the cabin came a cough, then another, and another. All eyes were trained on the doorway in anticipation of either a violent explosion or the imminent surrender of those concealed within.

XV

A dagger abruptly flew from the smoky room and bounced across the Orison's deck. It was immediately snatched up by one of the waiting pirates. The indistinct sounds of someone stirring inside the compartment could be heard and, moments later, a figure stepped from the murk and was silhouetted in the open doorway. A murmur rippled through the mob of cutthroats.

The occupant of the cabin was female.

Roughly grasping her arms, two louts on either side of the doorway flung the woman out of the cabin, into the center of the encircling pirates. Terrified, she stood trembling before her captors.

The young woman possessed delicate features and appeared to be about twenty years old. Tresses of blonde hair tumbled over her shoulders. Her skin was smooth and fair and her eyes, wide with fright, were green. The front of the linen smock that graced her willowy frame was spotted with the blood from the wound she had previously inflicted on the impetuous pirate.

"Who be you?" demanded the self-ordained leader of the group, an especially repellant pirate named Rashid. "How many others be with you?"

"I am Robin Goss, daughter to the master of this benign vessel," she softly responded.

"Her master lies bleeding like a stuck pig, along with her worthless crew," Rashid smirked. "How many be with you?"

"None. I was alone in my cabin."

Upon hearing this, one of the men ducked into the compartment and re-emerged holding the keg of gunpowder. The container was all but empty because, in rolling, it had disbursed most of its contents harmlessly along the deck. Not realizing this and fearing an imminent explosion, the prisoner elected to capitulate.

"Someone fetch Ling," suggested one of the men.

"No," countermanded Rashid. "We shall deal with this ourselves."

Smith began to feel uneasy. He feared to contemplate the fate of such a prize at the hands of his barbarous shipmates.

Rashid stepped closer to their captive. "Then it was you, alone, who slew Jameson," he wheedled.

"I slew an armed trespasser. Can you vouchsafe as compelling an excuse for slaying all these innocent men?" She gestured toward the lifeless bodies heaped about her.

Rashid ignored her challenge. "Your crime cannot go unpunished." Grinning, he extended a goatish hand and began to stroke her hair as his lecherous shipmates crowded nearer.

"Leave her alone." Smith's low warning was distinctly audible above the shuffling of the restive pirates.

Startled, all eyes shifted to the interloper. Rashid wheeled to face the assemblage.

"Who spoke?" he snarled.

Smith stood only a few feet away. "I did. Leave her alone, Rashid. She's only a child."

Rashid stared incredulously at Smith. "I know you only by sight. But unless you keep your tongue in your head, you and my sword will become inseparable." The throng began to murmur and Smith suddenly realized their growing aggressiveness was directed at him.

"The girl is defenseless. Her father and the rest of the crew are dead. Spare her further anguish." Smith attempted to appeal to Rashid's sense of compassion and morality, unaware that he possessed neither.

"Mark me," Rashid said, unmoved, as he turned back toward the captive. The atmosphere seethed with tension.

Rashid placed his hands on the shoulders of the terrified girl and resumed toying with her thick curls. The increasingly aroused mob pressed closer.

Smith repeated his warning but Rashid appeared not to hear.

Rashid's hands drifted to the straps that supported his captive's simple dress.

Smith, indifferent to the danger, stepped quickly forward and clamped a hand on Rashid's shoulder. Although the latter was shorter than Smith, he outweighed him by at least twenty pounds. Never-the-less, Smith spun the pirate around to face him as though he were a flyweight.

"Leave her alone."

Rashid's eyes blazed with fury and angry rumblings swelled from the surrounding horde. Seconds later, a pair of cutlasses were tossed into the clearing.

Rashid snatched up one of the blades and, without pausing, slashed at Smith. Smith jumped rearward to avoid Rashid's assault, but the partisan crowd roughly shoved him back toward his aggressor.

Leaping across the small field of combat, Smith managed to grab the remaining cutlass before Rashid renewed his attack. Then, weapons held at the ready, each man slowly circled the other, eyes fiercely intent. A breathless hush fell over the assembled crowd.

Rashid sprang toward Smith and deftly swung his cutlass diagonally downward from right to left. By leaning away Smith was able to elude the blow, though his defensive movement provoked disapproving hisses from the spectators. Encouraged by this token of support, Rashid charged forward again, but this time his onrush was rendered ineffectual by the unwavering point of Smith's cutlass. It was Rashid who now found it necessary to dodge another's steel; he retreated and resumed stalking Smith. For a few seconds the two men continued to circle one another.

Smith quickly reasoned that Rashid's bulk would prove an impediment if he were forced to maneuver quickly and repeatedly. His opponent's heaviness seemed to be Smith's only advantage, for he could not hope to elude the pirate's attacks indefinitely.   Neither could he physically overpower Rashid.

Without warning, Smith stepped directly into the path of his circling opponent and attempted to slash Rashid's legs.   Surprised by the abruptness and apparent folly of this action, Rashid easily blocked the cutlass' blow with his own, though in doing so he was forced to retreat another half-step.   Seizing the offensive momentum, Smith lunged at Rashid and, in the same motion, again chopped at him. Once more, Rashid was forced swiftly rearward in order to avoid Smith's sword, although he had little trouble in doing so. Because of Smith's unorthodox offense, however, Rashid was unable to reciprocate with an assault of his own for, as quickly as he had blocked one slash, Smith had delivered two more. Thus, Rashid was constantly forced out of position by the more aggressive Smith. Although the latter's blows were not overpowering, they rained down with such rapidity as to render a sortie impossible.

Thus, the duel continued.   The blows which cascaded from the seemingly indefatigable Smith were as from a man possessed.

Smith's limbs grew leaden from the number of slashes he made at his opponent in unbroken succession and perspiration streamed down his face, but still he attacked Rashid, still he lunged. For his part, the pirate backpedaled furiously under the onslaught, successfully diverting every blow but lacking any opportunity to attack.

Smith pushed the beleaguered Rashid around the small clearing formed by the circle of freebooters, depriving the pirate of the opportunity to establish solid footing in his backward retreat. Their fascinated shipmates watched as the clangs and rings of steel meeting steel filled the air.

"I'll kill you," spat Rashid through gritted teeth as Smith lunged at him. The panting, exhausted Smith responded with another swipe of his saber.

At that moment, as the overwhelmed Rashid stepped to his left to avoid being slashed, he caught his heel on the instep of one of the pirates who crowded too close to the struggle. Because of his weight and momentum, the heavy Rashid crashed to the deck amid the horrified gasps of his brethren. The careless onlooker instantly withdrew the offending foot. Too late: Rashid lay sprawled at the point of Smith's cutlass.

Still clutching his sword, Rashid slashed wildly upward while he unsuccessfully attempted to clamber to his feet. Smith was completely enervated and reluctant to continue, but the bestial expression in Rashid's eyes made it clear that he intended that Smith would not survive the contest.

Realizing that his strength was diminishing with each passing moment and that, once back on his feet, Rashid would be impossible to defeat, Smith was forced into a fateful decision.

Hesitating no longer, he advanced as close to the crouching Rashid as he dared and pressed him with spirited swordplay. Because of his awkward squatting position, Rashid was unable to effectively employ his cutlass, especially against the taller and fleeter Smith, who attacked with desperate vigor. Clumsily swinging his weapon in a wide haphazard arc while frantically scrambling away from his tormentor, Rashid's neck was momentarily exposed.

Before the pirate could assume a defensive posture, Smith strode forward and plunged his steel into Rashid's throat. The pirate realized his fatal mistake as the cutlass severed his windpipe.

Hunched on the Orison's deck, gasping for breath, Rashid plaintively searched the faces of his stunned comrades. His fingers opened, unbidden, and his blade tumbled to the deck with a thud.

Drenched with perspiration and trembling from exhaustion, Smith watched with relief as the pirate sprawled onto his back, gazing with sightless eyes at the burnished sky overhead.

XVI

"Holla! What is this?" Ling's harsh voice cut through the stagnant air, startling Smith, who stood panting near Rashid's body.

All heads jerked around as the hulking first-mate loomed upon the crowd. Like fearful children, the throng fell away as Ling strode into the center clearing, where his eyes fell upon the corpse that lay crumpled on deck and the crewman who stood over it, clutching a bloody cutlass. Ling's accusative gaze flashed over the nervous faces that surrounded him before coming to rest on Smith.

"You killed him?" Ling's eyes sparked with anger and Smith took an unconscious step rearward under their glare.

"I did not start the altercation. Rashid challenged and then attacked me...I simply defended myself in a fair fight."

"And who is this wench?" Ling demanded, nodding toward the girl who now stood at the extremity of the clearing.

"A prisoner. We found her while searching the cabins," nervously volunteered one of the onlookers.

"Though she is doubtless a prisoner, I suspect that such an insignificant slattern required little effort to ensnare," said Ling. He turned from Smith and approached the woman. "'What is your name and what are you doing aboard this ship?"

Fearlessly, the beautiful prisoner met Ling's basilisk-like stare as she replied, "My name is Robin Goss. My father was master of the Orison. I am aboard because my father was taking me to Lutetia, where he secured for me the position as companion to Madame de Cintre'."

"How much will she pay for your life?"

"Nothing, I suspect. I am not yet in her official employ and can be replaced without difficulty," answered Robin Goss, stoically.

Ling studied her impassively for a few seconds before turning to face the assembled pirates.

"Who will corroborate this man's account of what occurred? All here were witness to the killing. Which of you will speak his mind, for either the dead cries out for rightful vengeance or the victor demands approbation for a worthy deed. Which shall it be?"

No one in the throng spoke, though all glanced uneasily at one another like guilty schoolboys; none desired to become a party to whatever would prove the culmination of the duel.

Finally, Smith quietly said, "As I explained, Rashid attacked me and I was forced to defend myself. I had no wish to kill him, but his enraged state made any other action impossible."

"Shut up!" barked Ling so loudly that all jumped. "I see before me, sprawled in a pool of his own bile, a veteran of many campaigns whose skill with the blade was famed. I hear an easy tale that his death was wrought by the blade of a compatriot, though one new to the Harpy and assuredly not as adept in the use of the sword. There is an inconstancy here that demands explication, for methinks that some perfidy is afoot. Attend to me," he continued, rotating on his heel to face the entire crowd. "The hold of this ship brims with goods and comestibles that we must place aboard the Harpy. Whoever solves the puzzle of Rashid's death shall receive his share of booty, as well as his own."

At this declaration subdued murmurings broke out among the agitated crew. After a moment, the man over whose carelessly-placed foot Rashid had tripped stepped haltingly forward.

"I saw what happened," he began. He glanced nervously at the anxious faces ringing him. "Rashid was me mate and I have nothing to gain by lying. The fact is, this 'ere tart was holed-up in a cabin. She had already split one of our men when Rashid flushed her out." As the man talked, his speech became more and more rapid as the words tumbled out. "Rashid was in the process of questioning her when he," the man pointed to Smith, "jumped him. Rashid had just managed to free his blade when he slit him, and that's how it ended. I don't know what caused him to attack poor Rashid; the man just seemed to go mad."

"That's a lie!" cried Smith, but he knew that Rashid was a redoubtable figure aboard the Harpy with many allies among its crew. Moreover, Smith was a newcomer aboard the corsair and still considered an outsider. "Rashid attacked me first...I only defended myself. Rashid tripped over *his* foot and that's what led to his death. This man is only trying to foist the blame onto me!" But Smith's protestation fell on ears already predisposed to scorn him.

"As I suspected," Ling chuckled. "Put both the assassin and the wench in the Orison's brig." The brig aboard the Harpy was already tenanted by three condemned men, though none would be flung overboard until the vessel returned to the open sea. "Tonight, after our work is finished, she shall provide us some amusement. Perhaps that will give you wretches some incentive to bend your backs," he laughingly roared. And, indeed, he had good cause to laugh, for he had just gained for himself Smith's share of the Orison's plunder as well as a rare evening's entertainment.

Smith and Robin were both roughly laid upon and conveyed below deck, to the Orison's bleak cell. They could still hear Ling's booming laugh and the excited babble of tongues as the pirates began to transfer goods from the Orison to the waiting hold of the Harpy.

XVII

Even in the Orison's lightless brig, located below the vessel's waterline, Smith and Robin were able to hear the dissolute revelry taking place above them on the deck of the adjoining pirate ship. The freighter remained tied to the Harpy because nightfall prevented the pirates from completely stripping the Orison of all her useful accoutrements. On the morrow they would complete their plunder, whereupon the vessel's dead hulk would be cut free of the Harpy and flaming arrows launched onto her deck, converting the Orison into a crematorium before she slipped beneath the waves. Simply one more ill-starred vessel lost at sea.

But, for the nonce, the pirates drank, sang, laughed, and cast lots to see who would be the first to enjoy Robin Goss' favors later that night. Even the ancient captain emerged from his lair to quaff rum in celebration.

Their captors flung Smith and Robin into the Orison's brig without bothering to fetter them. Accordingly, the two prisoners sat in the darkness on rough wooden planks, deep in the bowels of the ship. Robin was silent though, earlier, she had wept long and painfully, and had spoken at length of her father and her life. Both prisoners fully understood that, very soon, Robin would be taken aboard the Harpy for the pleasure of its inebriated crew.

"We must try to escape," Smith said into the blackness.

A long silence ensued. Then, "It is impossible. We are as lost as my father and his crew." She spoke so softly as to be almost inaudible.

"Maybe, but I didn't come this far just to get pitched into the sea...if I go, I intend to take somebody with me."

"You will undoubtedly take me."

"No, that's not what I mean. I mean one of the crew. Ling, ideally. You know what I meant."

"It makes no difference. There is no hope." Robin began to sob quietly.

Smith stood and felt his way to the brig's door. Grasping its handle, he gently rattled it then began to vigorously yank on it. The door didn't yield.

For the first time, Smith began to panic and struggled to remain calm. He frantically strained against the door but it remained fast.

For what seemed countless hours Smith struggled with the brig's recalcitrant door, though it rebuffed all his efforts. Even if he managed to breach it, Smith had no idea what to do at that point, since the Harpy's deck teemed with hostile pirates. He simply concluded that he'd cross that bridge when he came to it.

Finally, completely enervated, Smith abandoned his pointless labors and lay quietly while he reevaluated their plight. Streams of perspiration flowed into his eyes, stinging them. His hair and now abundant beard clung to his face and, presently, he began to shiver as the damp air of the brig enveloped and chilled him.

After he had lain silently for a time, Robin spoke again. "Are you there?"

Even under the circumstances, Smith could not repress a slight smile, for where else could he be?

"Yes, I'm here," he assured her. For several minutes both remained quiet. Smith's ragged breathing gradually yielded to more normal respiration as he lay, unmoving.

Then, from beyond the bolted door, came the sound of stealthy footfalls on the descending stairs. In an instant, Smith's body tensed and his eyes grew wide as he strained to peer through the opacity toward the sound.

"What is it?" Robin whispered, for she, too, heard the approaching footsteps.

"Shhhhh," breathed Smith, though he entertained no doubt that it was Ling coming to claim his beautiful captive. Straining his ears as well as his eyes, he tried to isolate the sound, but the pounding of his heart was all he heard. Perspiration again flooded his face and hands, which had grown icy.

After the muted rattling of its lock, the cell door opened with a slight squeak. Because the outside stairwell was unlit, however, Smith was unable to discern the identity of the intruder. Robin made no sound, for she lay motionless and unbreathing, tensely staring toward the doorway. The hollow sound of muffled steps filled the cramped room as the anonymous stranger entered the brig.

"It's me, Peter," whispered a stunning voice, "Are you there, Smith?"

The pent-up anxiety that gripped Smith burst like a wave of nausea.

"Yes, yes, I'm here," he managed to gasp.

"And the girl?"

"Yes, we're both here."

"We must act quickly...Ling will come for her very soon." Peter spoke rapidly as he felt his way to Smith's berth in the blackness. "If you quietly steal your way along the deck to the davits, you will be able to lower a life boat and make your escape," he instructed as he gripped Smith's arm.

"Why are you doing this?" asked Smith, incredulously, as he closed his stiff fingers around Peter's hand.

"Because I am obligated to you. By liberating you, my debt is absolved. But I can only release you from your present captivity. You must, yourselves, flee the Orison if you entertain any hope of survival. I can assist you no further."

"Where did you get the key?"

"On a peg outside the door. The guard assigned by Ling deserted his post in order to take part in the celebration aboard the Harpy. In his absence I availed myself of the key. But ask me nothing further. You and the girl must fly from the ship while you still can."

"Ling will surely punish you, Peter."

The other man shook his head in the darkness. "Ling will have no reason to suspect that I assisted your escape. The same cannot be said for your guard, however, who will soon find himself occupying a slat in the Harpy's brig."

"I am sincerely sorry for him," Smith said.

Peter softly scoffed. "Your sympathy is misplaced, Smith, for the man assigned by Ling to guard you tonight was none other than Gamez."

"Gamez? Who is he?"

"The one who denounced you to Ling by claiming that you attacked Rashid unprovoked."

Smith chuckled. "So, I guess there *is* a god, eh, Peter? But, even though Gamez lied about what happened today, he doesn't deserve to die."

He couldn't see Peter shrug in the blackness. "It is a matter of indifference to Ling. In fact, Ling will profit from your escape, for he will now take his share, your share, Rashid's share, *and* Gamez's share of the booty. By escaping, you will have done Ling an unintentional favor."

Smith hopped off the board on which he'd been lying and hurriedly moved to Robin. Peter returned to the doorway and peered upward, toward the Orison's deck.

"No one is coming. Be quick and get away," he whispered. "I must go now." He began to ascend the stairs, then turned back. "If you find your way back to Asem, locate my wife and tell her that I still live, and that my thoughts are always of her." In an instant Peter was gone.

Smith gently helped Robin slide off her plank and onto the floor. Sensation speedily returned to her stiff limbs and Smith grasped Robin's arm and hastened her toward the brig's open doorway. He gingerly stuck his head out.

"The coast is clear," he whispered.

The pair cautiously began to ascend the stairwell, Robin pressing close to Smith. Seconds later, they emerged onto the Orison's deck.

Directly across the narrow gap that separated the two creaking vessels, torches soaked in whale oil cast a harsh light on a scene of boisterous merrymaking aboard the Harpy. Pirates brawled, sang boisterously, and laughed uproariously. Several men lay unconscious in pools of vomit, too weak to rise from where they had collapsed in drunken stupors. Other sailors swilled rum from wooden casks appropriated from what had once been part of the Orison's consignment of cargo.

Smith slowly emerged from the mouth of the stairwell, where he crouched. No one aboard the Harpy looked in his direction or appeared to take notice of him, so he motioned for Robin to follow. Fearfully, she emerged from the protective shadows.

"We must reach the life boats over there," he whispered, pointing to the Harpy's port side. Robin nodded, swallowed, and placed a trembling hand in Smith's. They began to crab their way toward a section of the Orison's railing farthest from the Harpy.

The two escapees neared the railing, beyond which the Orison's three lifeboats were suspended from davits. Smith was hopeful that each boat carried several day's provisions.

He glanced about the immediate area to confirm they remained unobserved by any pirates who might still be lingering aboard the freighter. The deck had previously been cleared of the casualties from that morning's combat through the simple expedient of stripping their bodies and dumping them overboard.

From where they crouched, Smith had an unobstructed view across the Orison's empty deck onto the brightly illuminated Harpy, where he spotted Peter standing with a group of shipmates. Their eyes locked only an instant before Peter looked away. He heartily slapped one of his compatriots on the back and took a long draught from a bottle of rum.

Talking and laughing about nothing in particular, Peter began ambling toward a spot on the far side of the deck. His drunken companions stumbled after him.

Smith grabbed Robin's hand and, together, they sprinted the remaining distance to the railing. In mere seconds they scaled it and settled into the swaying lifeboat.

"Keep your head down," cautioned Smith, for he feared her pale skin would reflect like a beacon in the light from the Harpy's torches. Robin complied and hunched down in the bottom of the boat while Smith, with infinite care, released the central pulley that lowered the craft into the water, twenty feet below.

Smith snubbed the rope securing the lifeboat to one of its oarlocks and released only enough at a time to lower the craft a corresponding few inches. By keeping the control rope taut, he was thus able to control their descent. Although the rusted pulley squeaked as it rotated, the general clamor from the Harpy rendered the sound almost imperceptible. They had already dropped below the Orison's railing and each revolution of the pulley brought the lifeboat closer to the onyx surface of the Great Sea. The noise of raucous carousing aboard the Harpy was already greatly diminished because the Orison's bulk muted the clamor. Increasingly, the only sound was the soft lapping of water against her hull.

"Hold on, hold on," whispered Smith, mostly to himself, as he continued to release rope. Robin said nothing.

Minutes, hours, or eons later, the lifeboat's gradual descent suddenly ceased as it at last settled onto the black water. Smith released the remainder of his control rope and ran it through the pulley far above them and into the lifeboat, where he coiled it. No angry faces appeared over the railing, no excited shouts heralding their escape rent the air. Even the din of the revelry taking place only a few yards on the other side of the Orison could barely be heard as Smith used an oar to carefully push their lifeboat away from the freighter. In the gloom, the only distinct sounds were the tiny wavelets thumping against its fragile shell.

Silently, Smith slipped the oars into their locks and began to row into the featureless ebon immensity of the Great Sea, far from the pirate vessel and its noxious crew.

XVIII

A fiery glow on the horizon heralded sunrise and, minutes later, the flaming solar orb crept slowly from the waters of the Great Sea. Orange it was, and its blazing refulgence scattered darts of vivifying light upon the face of the deep. Upon two figures in a tiny row boat becalmed upon the measureless waters, it cast a warming embrace to banish the damp chill of night.

Smith leaned back to rest his shoulders and absorb the warmth; Robin lay curled in the bottom of the craft, sleeping. They had rowed all night, not knowing in which direction but anxious to distance themselves from the Harpy. Smith scanned the horizon; the pirate vessel was nowhere in sight. Neither the corsair, nor any other ship, was visible on the viridian expanse that enveloped them.

With a sigh, Smith leaned forward, grasped the oar handles with raw and blistered hands, and resumed rowing. Later on, he would wake Robin and they would eat from the provisions stored in the lifeboat. But he would row a while longer.

***

The comforting glow of the morning sun became a tyrannical scourge as the day wore on. When Robin awoke she insisted that Smith eat and rest while she rowed. He agreed only because his hands were cramping and it was only with great effort that he was able to remove them from the oars. Even so, his palms burned because the earlier blisters had broken to become oozing sores. Smith bolted down some of the dried fruit stored in the lifeboat and drank sparingly from a skin of fresh water.

"You eat now," he told Robin, for he knew that if he forestalled rowing for too long, his hands would stiffen and become useless claws. So saying, he switched places with her and wincingly clutched the oar handles once again. The oars lethargically slapped the water as the rowboat nosed forward.

"Have you any idea where we are?" asked Robin.

"None whatsoever. Maybe we can figure it out tonight when the stars come out." Smith's exposed skin was already starting to burn from the unrelenting sun and his eyes throbbed from the blinding glare that ricocheted off the water's surface. Robin, too, suffered. Through the whole of the day and into the cool dusk she talked quietly of the tempestuous circumstances that had recently disrupted her prosaic existence, their fortuitous escape from the Harpy, and her hope of reaching sanctuary. She regularly relieved Smith at the oars, urging that a rest of even brief duration was essential. She would then row without complaint until Smith insisted that she allow him to resume. In time, her hands became masses of raw flesh, even as Smith's already were.

Because they had no anchor it was not possible for their craft to remain fixed in position while they slept. At nightfall, as they huddled together in the bottom of the lifeboat in an effort to stay warm, the ineluctable currents of the Great Sea carried them far adrift. Smith had previously determined that sunset probably occurred in the western quarter of the compass, as it did in his normal world. But even armed with this information he didn't know in which direction the nearest land lay, and the strange constellations in the night sky offered no clue. So they rowed by day and slept by night, partaking of their supplies with the greatest thrift. Their large skin of fresh water, once plump, was now flaccid and rugose. They knew its contents would soon be depleted but neither spoke their fears aloud. On the contrary, Robin expressed her unwavering confidence of finding land. Smith was far less sanguine.

In the late afternoon of their third day at sea, having seen no other living creatures except a school of sunfish basking at the surface, the discordant squawk of a seagull pierced the stagnant air. Smith, who was resting at the oars, was instantly galvanized and searched the cloudless sky, seeking its source. He shaded his eyes against the glare and, a moment later, was rewarded by the sight of a gannet circling high above. Even as he watched, the bird folded its wings against its sides and plunged seaward...seconds later it crashed into the sea a few yards from the lifeboat before emerging with a struggling argent fish in its beak. At this, a cacophony of shrieks and squeals burst through the air as other birds, observing the good fortune of their rival, converged upon him from seemingly empty air to steal his prize.

"Robin, look!" Smith cried to his companion, who was dozing fitfully.

Robin drew herself erect. "What's wrong?" she asked, spiritlessly.

"Nothing! Look at the birds! Look! We can't be too far from land!"

Robin scanned the sky overhead. A multitude of gannets and terns now swooped above the craft or skimmed along the surface of the water. Some rode atop small swells and the air was alive with their noisy chatter.

"How far are we from land?" she asked, excited, though the horizon remained bereft of any discernable shoreline.

"I don't know. I don't even know in which direction it is, but I'm sure we must be fairly close with all these birds around. I think we should just ride the current and hope that it carries us landward. What do you think, Robin?"

"If you believe that to be the best thing to do, then I agree with all my heart. I confess total ignorance of nautical matters and trust your good judgment."

Smith plied the oars in order to augment the easy movement of the current. Robin strained her eyes forward but saw no land.

***

The sizzling ferocity of the sun was quenched as it began to slip beneath the moderating waters of the Great Sea. In ever increasing numbers, sea birds besieged their small boat, which had lately entered an area of prolific aquatic plant growth. Smith was heartened by this and expressed his confidence to Robin.

"Look! Look!" she enthusiastically blurted as she pointed over Smith's shoulder. Smith feathered the oars and craned his neck toward the object of Robin's excitement. Far across the darkening waters could be seen the black silhouette of a landmass rising from the sea.

"Excellent," Smith grinned. "I hope the tide will pull us closer. Do you care to hazard a guess as to where we are?"

"I fear I do not know, but whatever land it is, it must be preferable to our present condition."

"No doubt." Smith looked around in an effort to orient himself. To starboard, the sun was already half consumed by the waters of the Great Sea, so he reasoned that the landmass to which they were heading lay generally southward. He didn't know whether they were close to Asem, Jmar, or Kaelops, or far removed from all of them. Of the disposition and whereabouts of the Harpy he was also unaware, though he was reasonably certain the corsair had discontinued pursuit of them if, indeed, any such attempt had been undertaken in the first place. All that Smith knew for a certainty is that they must head straightaway toward the unknown landmass, where their prospects for survival would presumably be better.

Smith reassumed control of the oars and eagerly began rowing landward, ignoring the searing pain in his shoulders and arms. For herself, Robin could barely contain her excitement. In the gathering dusk Smith feared losing sight of the enigmatic landmass.

"Do you see a light anywhere?" he asked as he steadily rowed, apprehensive that, if they failed to locate a beach where they could land before nightfall, their tiny boat might be dashed to pieces upon shoals.

"No, we are still too distant. Perhaps as we draw closer I shall be able to see more clearly."

Smith continued to row, although his initial optimism of securing imminent landfall was slowly becoming displaced by pangs of uneasiness. Still, he did not falter, for he knew that this could well be their only opportunity for salvation.

***

It seemed as though he'd been rowing for hours when Robin cried, "Arthur! I see a light on shore! Look!"   Smith turned.

Through the gloom he could discern a yellowish pinpoint shimmering across the sea. Although he could barely see Robin in the darkness, there was no mistaking the cynosure that glimmered slightly to their left.

"I'll head toward it as best I can," Smith assured her. "Keep an eye on it and tell me if I stray too far." With that, he settled back and, with a sigh, began rowing decisively toward the beacon, hoping that it marked an area of safe harborage. After a time, they switched places and he acted as navigator.

Despite their fatigue, they rowed through the night. By alternately taking turns at the oars, they eventually drew nigh the landmass. When the sky finally began to lighten, Smith, who was rowing, slumped tiredly and allowed the lifeboat to drift shoreward on choppy wavelets.   Scores of curious seabirds swarmed them.

The horseshoe-shaped inlet toward which they glided was craggy and densely forested.   Their small craft floated into a natural harbor formed by two encircling promontories.

Before them stretched a curved black-sand beach.   What lay beyond it could only be guessed.

XIX

Smith used the oars to steer the lifeboat toward the center of the beach. When the water grew sufficiently shallow, he climbed from the craft and manually pushed it onward. Once its keel began to scrape, Robin, too, jumped into the shallows and assisted in dragging the lifeboat clear of the water, well above the tideline.

They both collapsed upon the sand, utterly exhausted.

The beach extended from the shoreline a distance of only fifty yards. Immediately beyond it was a morass of mangrove trees surmounted by beetling scarp.

Smith abruptly sat up. "Look there," he said, pointing toward the top of the nearest bluff. Far up its side, almost obscured by trees, peered the facade of a tiny building.

Robin followed his gaze. "A dwelling?"

"Looks like one. Maybe it was the source of the light we saw last night."

"Someone lives there?" Because of its distance, they could discern no activity around the structure.

Smith shrugged. "I don't know, but that light had to come from *somewhere*. I think we should find some shade and rest for a while. Afterward, we'll scrounge some food and fresh water and decide what we should do going forward."

"Agreed. Neither of us has truly rested since escaping the Harpy and, for myself, am so tired that I can scarcely think clearly."

Smith and Robin trudged exhaustedly across the beach toward the mangroves and quickly located a dry, shaded area. Smith stretched full length and yawned while Robin sank in a heap against the trunk of a tree.

"I don't think I've ever been more exhausted," he said, closing his eyes. Robin smiled wanly.

"Please stay exactly as you are and do not move."

The startling voice emerged from the bushes near them, causing both Smith and Robin to involuntarily jump. Neither expected to encounter anyone on what appeared to be a deserted beach.

Defying the command, Smith sat up and looked about in an effort to determine the exact location of the disembodied voice, his mind racing. Before he could formulate a course of action, however, an individual brandishing an old-fashioned blunderbuss stepped from behind the thick shrubbery.

Robin turned to look at Smith, her eyes wide with fear.

The interloper, who appeared somewhat younger than Smith, was clad in what was manifestly some sort of uniform. Though clean, it was well-worn and frayed in spots. He skeptically surveyed the two unkempt fugitives.

"Who are you and what are you doing here?" he demanded.

Smith glanced at Robin before replying. "My name is Arthur Smith and this is my daughter, Robin. We are survivors of an attack at sea. The vessel on which we were passengers was set upon by pirates and plundered. Although we managed to escape, we were adrift in a lifeboat until reaching these shores. It is entirely thanks to a merciful providence that the sea conveyed us here."

The man listened attentively to Smith's recitation. "What was the name of your vessel?"

"The Orison."

"Where was she bound?"

"To Jmar from Kaelops." Smith did not know if this was true, but hoped it sounded credible.

"How long have you been adrift?"

"Three days," replied Smith.

"May I ask where we are?" Robin interjected.

The man fidgeted momentarily though his weapon remained trained on them.

"You are in the Federated Monarchy of Valh and I am obligated to inform you that you both are under arrest for espionage."

"What!" burst both Robin and Smith, spontaneously.

"Until your story can be corroborated you will remain guests of the Monarchy. I sincerely apologize for further compounding your ills, though you may be assured that no harm will come to you if you cooperate."

Robin could not mask her scorn. "'Guests!' What is the meaning of this outrage?" she demanded. "We scarcely manage to escape with our lives from an attack on our ship, spend days drifting helplessly upon the sea, and when we finally reach safety are seized for a crime we have no knowledge of and certainly did not commit. I implore you to leave us in peace, sir."

"I am truly sorry, but these are precarious times. We are forced to adopt measures that we would, under ordinary circumstances, eschew. Regrettably, all are made to suffer the consequences, the guilty and innocent alike."

"Why are things so precarious?" Smith probed.

"Because of the hostilities that currently exist between the principalities of Nevid and Valh."

"We know nothing of such hostilities for, as I stated, we are strangers here."

"I would fain trade my knowledge for your ignorance," responded the man. "But I beg you to accompany me to my headquarters, where you may rest until your identities and intentions can be confirmed. While I am inclined to believe you, I must caution you not to attempt an escape, as my duty in this matter is clear."

With this warning, their interrogator gestured menacingly with the blunderbuss. "Come please; there is a path over there."

Smith sighed audibly. Taking Robin's arm, they began trudging in the direction indicated. Their captor followed closely behind.

The trail on which they plodded was well worn and very quickly began ascending the face of the cliff.

After walking only a few minutes Smith concluded that it undoubtedly terminated at the modest structure they had previously observed from the beach.

In less than three-quarters of an hour they stood before it.

XX

"Enter, please," gestured their unsought host.

Smith and Robin stepped through the low doorway. Inside the one-room bungalow was a cot, a rickety chair, a wood-burning stove, and a small chest of drawers. Although austere, the interior was neat and orderly.   Brilliant sunlight flooded the room through two seaward-facing windows on either side of the entry.

"You live alone here?" Robin asked.

"My headquarters is only one league distant and I remain in constant contact." The man removed a leather bag from a hook on the wall and slipped its strap over his shoulder. "Indeed, we shall be there presently."

"What is your name?"

"I am Scout First-Class Bread." He led them outside, where another trail snaked from the tiny outpost, and carefully secured the cottage's door,

The trio walked along the path in single file and quickly crested a nearby bluff. Their guard, who still clutched his weapon, was breathing heavily.

"Please sit on the ground," he instructed between gulps of air as he removed the bag from his shoulder.

"What do you intend to do with us?" asked Robin, nervously.

"I must appraise headquarters of your presence and inform them that we are en route."

From his bag Bread removed a heliostat and began casting a signal to an adjacent ridge. Seconds later, a terse acknowledgement flashed from its summit.

"A runner has been dispatched to announce your apprehension. Do not fear for your safety, as my commander is an honorable man. He will listen to you with complete neutrality. The facts as you relate them can be easily verified and, if true, you will be set at liberty with our apologies. To the extent it is within our power, we will also assist you back to your homeland."

Smith nodded mechanically and climbed to his feet. The two men helped Robin to stand, whereupon Smith asked, "Where, exactly, are your headquarters?"

"Yonder," replied Bread, pointing toward the valley at the bottom of the escarpment. "Because it lies in a natural declivity it remains hidden from sight." The contours of a distant settlement were faintly visible on the horizon.

"That's your headquarters?" Smith enquired.

"No," replied Bread. "That is Thule. Thule and Jmar are the largest cities in the monarchy, though Jmar is in the larger."

Smith's interest was immediately piqued at the mention of the latter, as he recalled the Harpy's recent sojourn there.

"How far are they from here?" he blandly inquired.

"Both are five leagues distant, or thereabouts. My headquarters are situated more-or-less halfway between them."

"Is the River Omer nearby?" Smith probed.

"It is not far. But please forestall further questions until we arrive at my headquarters. Come, let us resume." Together, the trio recommenced their descent to the valley below.

Smith rejoiced at learning that the Omer was apparently nearby. Assuming he managed to extricate himself and Robin from their present imbroglio, he would try to navigate the Omer upriver to rejoin his friends, the gnomes.

***

In a little over half an hour, Robin, Smith, and Scout First-Class Bread stood before the weathered door of the post commander. Bread's modest headquarters were nothing more than a cluster of small whitewashed buildings surrounded on three sides by poplar trees. The fourth side was open, save for a hedgerow with a wooden gate and sentry box. A compact dirt lane extended from the compound to the surrounding woodland.

Bread adjusted his frayed uniform and rapped smartly upon the door.

"Come in," boomed a hearty voice from within.

The scout opened the door and motioned his two captives forward. A portly, grey-haired man stood from behind a desk as they entered the room.

"Scout First-Class, Bread, reporting," he announced.

"Greetings, Bread," the man smiled. He quickly arranged four chairs in a group and invited all to sit. "I am Commander Tomkins," he said, soberly, after all had been seated. "I understand that you two have come to us under rather peculiar circumstances. Kindly acquaint me with the particulars of your late misadventures, if you will."

Smith introduced himself and reiterated that Robin was his daughter. He then repeated the essential details of their travails. The commander and Bread listened without interrupting.

When Smith concluded his abbreviated recital, the commander spoke. "We know that a merchantman bearing the name 'Orison' is overdue in Jmar. Our intelligence network keeps us informed of such things. It is presumed that she was attacked and sunk by freebooters, as you relate, because the Great Sea swarms with marauders and such attacks are by no means uncommon. Your account is plausible and I am convinced of its truthfulness. Moreover, neither of you have the appearance of spies. I am sincerely sorry for the grievous loss of your ship and her crew."

Commander Tomkins then turned to Bread, whose vigilance and constancy he lavishly praised, notwithstanding that his captives proved to be innocuous.

"I feel especially compelled to express sympathy to your daughter," said the commander to Smith, "for the recent outrages she has been forced to endure. I beg you to allow us to redeem ourselves, at least to a modest degree, by assisting you in the completion of your journey. It will be our honor."

Smith started to reply but was interrupted by a tumult of shrill curses and angry imprecations alternating with other, less strident voices, from outside the premises. The intensity of the obvious quarrel amplified as the squabble drew nearer the commander's office. A sense of foreboding gripped Smith as he attempted to isolate the abusive, screeching tone of the primary disputant.

Commander Tomkins shot to his feet and strode to the door to determine the source of the commotion.

Before he reached it, the door flew open and a seedy figure swept into the room, closely followed by the pair of soldiers whom Smith and Robin encountered at the compound's sentry box upon their arrival. Horrified astonishment surged over Smith at the sight of the diabolical alchemist.

"Lasceaux!" he spat.

"What is going on here?" barked Tomkins. "What is the meaning of this intrusion? And who is this bundle of rags?" he demanded of the sheepish guards, indicating Smith's nemesis.

"I am Lasceaux," the alchemist imperiously proclaimed, "and am here to unmask this poseur and undeceive you as to his true identity."

Smith and Robin sprang to their feet. Tomkins ignored the blustering alchemist and again addressed the soldiers who stood mutely behind Lasceaux.

"How is it that this individual is able to enter this compound and burst into my office completely unhindered?"

"He was adamant and half mad. We attempted to stop him but he rebuffed us and made his way here before we could summon reinforcements," one of the sentries meekly explained.

Smith's chimeric hope that the alchemist had wearied of his single-minded pursuit was, in a stroke, exposed as nothing more than wishful thinking. The vile serpent stood before them, though now his head was uncovered, revealing patches of black hair atop his misshapen skull.

The alchemist addressed himself directly to the commander. "My advent, though turbulent, was entirely warranted for, as you shall see, no quarter must be allowed your perfidious guests."

Tomkins skeptically assessed Lasceaux.

"Indeed? That is a most interesting revelation. While I would ordinarily not tolerate such a scandalous intrusion, under the circumstances I will hear you in the interest of ascertaining the facts in this curious matter. You are entirely unknown to me, sir, and I know only as much of my guests as they have deigned to reveal. I caution you, however, that the intelligence you declare to possess merits your trespass, else I shall have you thrown from this compound."

The commander advanced threateningly toward Lasceaux, whom Smith was amazed to observe actually retreat a step. King Gob's statement was confirmed: Lasceaux was, indeed, vulnerable when removed from his element.

"Mark me," the alchemist croaked as he pointed a skeletal finger at Smith, "That man is a fugitive from justice! Whatever fable he spun regarding his appearance here was a flagrant lie because he only recently absconded from a lawful arrest at sea.

Furthermore, he faithlessly defrauded another and was fleeing the consequences of *that* ignominy even before being convicted of murdering a ship's hand." Lasceaux's words bubbled from him as from a noxious caldron. "I beseech you to attend to me," he cackled.

Smith stood dumbfounded as he listened to the outrageous accusations hurled against him. Robin looked wildly from Lasceaux to Smith and back to Lasceaux. The soldiers hesitatingly moved toward Smith.

"Question him yourself! Truly, question him!" shrieked Lasceaux, fearing that his prize was about to slip through his fingers once again.

Tomkins responded, "No. I shall instead question you, Lasceaux, since you purport to know a great deal about my guests. As I previously informed you, I know only as much as they confided to me." He cast a glance at Smith that could not be interpreted, "Now, you insist that Smith is a fugitive from justice, correct?"

The alchemist visibly relaxed. "You apprehend most admirably," he smirked.

"And what is your interest in his capture? Are you a member of the constabulary?"

"In a manner of speaking. I have been tirelessly pursuing the knave for many weeks in the interest of those whom he has wronged. My sole concern resides in seeing justice done on their behalf."

"I see," said Tomkins, thoughtfully. "That is most praiseworthy." Smith and Robin listened in fearful silence but did not speak. "But who is the young lady?" continued the commander. "Was she a party to

Smith's misdeeds or simply his daughter, as he asserts?"

Lasceaux's eyes flicked toward Robin. "She is plainly his confederate, though I have little interest in her. I assure you, however, that she is not his daughter. Of that I am certain."

"Tell me, then, of Smith's escape at sea. He informs me that he fled a ship that was under attack by pirates. This was not so?"

"Ha! No, indeed! He escaped from the brig of a vessel resting at anchor."

"I see. Kindly refresh my memory: for what crime was he imprisoned?"

"For the murder of a shipmate."

"Inform me, sir, of the port where the ship was anchored when the fugitive effected his escape, as well as the identity of the vessel. The harbor-master's log will confirm the incident."

The alchemist fidgeted uneasily before responding. "I am uncertain of both the port and the ship's name."

The commander frowned. "Notwithstanding this lacuna, you presume to accuse my guest of appalling villainy? What was the registry of the vessel?"

"Registry?" asked Lasceaux, blankly.

"Registry: under what flag did she sail?"

Lasceaux shifted his weight from one foot to the other. "She sailed under her own flag," he finally responded.

"Truly? That is most unusual, for all lawful vessels with which I am acquainted sail under the protection of bona fide commonwealths, whose colors they invariably display. What was the nature of this peculiar vessel?"

Smith could discern the trend of the astute commander's perceptive questions. So, too, could the increasingly nervous alchemist, for he continued to fidget under the interrogation.

Lasceaux cleared his throat loudly and wiped his squamous head before replying. "A corsair."

"A corsair?" Tomkins raised a quizzical eyebrow. "It is your assertion that my guest was seized by pirates for killing one of their own?"

"Murder is murder," protested Lasceaux, hotly, "What difference does the identity of the unfortunate victim make?"

"Truly, 'murder is murder,' Tomkins concurred. "But you will agree with me that the killing of a pirate is hardly murder. Rather, it is a laudable act, akin to eliminating a dangerous, wild beast."

From behind Tomkins, Robin interjected, "Smith murdered no one. Nay, he protected my honor from a savage who intended to defile me. Such a deed is far from murder."

"I should say not!" exclaimed Tomkins. "Most particularly when the victim was a freebooter! I should rather applaud my guest than punish him," he chuckled.

"Your insouciance does you no credit," snarled the alchemist. There also remains the matter of the malicious fraud he perpetrated."

"And what were the circumstances of that egregious deception?" inquired Tomkins with a twinkle in his eye for, having perceived the essence of his grievances, the commander no longer took the squawking alchemist seriously.

"This man," raged Lasceaux while waving a trembling finger at Smith, "deliberately represented an object as something entirely different from what it actually was, to the grave detriment of his victim"

"Oh? What was the object at issue and whom did he beguile by means of this ruse?" Tomkins was now toying with the vitriolic alchemist.

Lasceaux, now livid, screeched, "A piece of fruit...he enticed someone into believing that an ordinary piece of fruit was in reality a lump of gold!" The alchemist was furious at the blithe manner in which the commander was treating his accusations.

Tomkins spontaneously burst into laughter. Smith, Robin, Bread, and the two guards also began to laugh, as much at Tomkins' mirthful reaction as Lasceaux's sputtering frustration.

"And dare I ask the identity of the simpleton duped into believing that a piece of fruit was a lump of gold?" chortled Tomkins.

"Smith's deceit was practiced upon me!" screamed the alchemist. "I demand that you surrender him to me without further hindrance. You may keep the female for your own amusement; I am interested only in Smith."

Lasceaux was, by this time, reduced to virtual pleading, though he strove to maintain a dignified façade. His strained hauteur only succeeded in provoking greater peals of laughter.

The commander turned to Smith. "Do you refute this rascal's accusations? Indeed, were you a brigand aboard a corsair?" he inquired.

"They are essentially true, and more besides," Smith freely conceded. "As for being a brigand, I was enslaved by pirates after having been drugged and all my possessions stolen."

"Then I beg you to accept my sincere compliments. This buffoon has excited more pleasure than I've enjoyed in a long time." Tomkins turned to the raging alchemist. "You, alone, are the author of your follies and have no cause to demand reparations from my guests. As promised, you were provided opportunity to voice your grievances and I find them utterly lacking. Accordingly, I order you to depart at once."

Commander Tomkins addressed the two guards who trailed Lasceaux into his office. "Escort this scoundrel to either the front gate or the guardhouse, whichever he finds most congenial."

Hearing these words of exoneration, Smith's and Robin's hearts leapt and broad smiles broke upon their faces. Lasceaux's eyes, however, narrowed as he stared at the trio. Sensing that further protest would be fruitless, he turned on his heel and brushed past the guards.

"See that he departs," Tomkins repeated. He then turned to Smith and Robin and asked simply, "Now, who was that individual and what is the nature of your dealings with him?"

Smith took a deep breath, glanced at Robin, who looked at him quizzically, and wearily resumed his seat.

Robin, Tomkins, and Bread listened keenly as he began to speak.

XXI

For a half-hour, Smith spoke without interruption of his adventures. His audience proved an attentive one for, until then, none knew the whole of his trials, especially those involving the pernicious alchemist. Smith revealed that Lasceaux abducted him for use in his noxious experiments but that, following his escape from the alchemist's lair, he was unable to return home. Smith forbore detailing his sojourn among the gnomes, fearing his listeners would find the particulars simply too fantastic for credence. Smith told of his passage down the River Omer to Asem, where he was drugged and crimped aboard the Harpy.

"I'm sorry to have deceived you," he rued, "but feared that if you learned that I'd served aboard a corsair, you'd have refused to help us. Or worse."

"In order to survive, one must perforce do disagreeable things," Tomkins observed. "To prefer life to death is only sensible."

Smith described the Harpy's attack on the Orison, the subsequent discovery of Robin, and the death of Rashid. He concluded his narrative by detailing their escape from the pirates and Peter's help in effecting it.

"Yours is a most astonishing tale and I commend you both on your enterprise and bravery," Tomkins affirmed when Smith had finished. "But now," he exclaimed, leaping to his feet, "let us see whether it is not too late to seize that devil."

He raced from the room, only to return a few minutes later. "The guards inform me the swine went directly out the compound gate and disappeared. I ordered a search party, but fear that he may have already gotten away. I'm profoundly sorry," he apologized as he resumed his seat.

"No need, Commander. I'm certain Lasceaux will not return." But even as he spoke, Smith now knew the tenacious alchemist would not be so easily rebuked.

"Given that you did not know how to find your way home, what was your goal when you escaped Lasceaux's laboratory?" Robin asked after a moment.

"My immediate objective was simply to elude him," Smith responded. "Secondly, I hoped to make my way to Kaelops, a place Lasceaux had spoken of, thinking that I might find someone there able to help me."

"I feel badly that I foolishly allowed the fiend to escape, and doubly so that I am powerless to help you return home," mourned the commander. He then brightened. "Perhaps, Robin, we can at least help *you* to return to your family's embrace. Alternatively, you are both welcome to reside with us for as long as you desire."

Robin looked pensively at Smith before responding. "I will remain with Arthur, wherever that may be. I have no family, for my father was a widower. And now he, too, is gone."

Smith reached out and took her slim hand in his. "Thank you for your kind offer, Commander. But we must reflect on our future plans.

"Of course, of course," Tomkins concurred.

Suddenly, Bread spoke. "There is a seer in Thule who is widely esteemed for his extraordinary wisdom. Perhaps he can help you." The others looked at Bread in startled surprise, causing him smile self-consciously. "Forgive me if I spoke out of turn, Commander."

Tomkins looked dubious but invited Bread to continue.

"I do not know whether this man's fame is warranted, but I have heard of his skill in locating lost persons and objects...perhaps he could locate Smith's home, as well."

"Harrumph," muttered Tomkins. "I am aware of this individual's reputation, Bread."

Smith briefly pondered Bread's revelation. "Like you, Commander, I've always been skeptical of such things. However, my recent experiences have, if nothing else, revealed that the universe is a far stranger place than I could ever possibly have imagined. The individual Bread speaks of, if genuine, might actually be able to offer advice about how to find my way home...there's certainly nothing to be lost by talking to him."

"His name is 'Luman'," Bread volunteered.

"Luman enjoys quite a reputation throughout the region," Tomkins acknowledged, "though for good or ill I cannot say.   However, I shall leave you to resolve for yourselves your future course. Whatever your decision, be assured of our wholehearted cooperation and assistance."

XXII

The following noontide, having slept, eaten, bathed, and changed into fresh clothes, Smith and Robin found themselves en route to Luman's habitation in a coach provided by Commander Tomkins. Bread was their driver and the commander also ordered another of his men to accompany them as escort, in the event the alchemist still lurked nearby.

As they traveled, Smith's mind was a jumble of chaotic thoughts. He did not know what future lay in store nor, indeed, whether Luman could help or would even grant them an audience. However, his most troubling thoughts concerned Robin, as he had no idea whether she could depart the present world and accompany him into his. Though Smith did not voice his anxieties to Robin, who sat beside him clutching his arm, he feared that such a transition might not be possible.

Robin broke the silence. "Do you believe the seer may be able to help you?"

"I hope so."

"I hope so, too." She fervently hugged his arm.

"Holla! What is this?" cried Bread as he drew the coach to a stop. Along the dusty roadway could be seen a lone individual, wearing a dark suit, ambling toward them. Smith felt a pang of fear but quickly discerned that the figure was not Lasceaux. Bread nudged the horses forward; their mounted escort followed closely.

As they drew abreast of the walker, Smith leaped incredulously out of his seat.

"Parsons!" He exclaimed.   His shout startled everyone, but especially the figure in the roadway.

"Arthur?" spoke the latter, hesitatingly.

"Parsons!" shouted Smith again, joyously. He bounded from the carriage and sped to the bewildered figure, whom he emotionally embraced. "How is it that you're here? I honestly can't believe my eyes!"

"Yes, it's me!" the man confirmed. "But where is this place and what are *you* doing here?" Smith could not stem the tears of joy that streamed down his cheeks. It seemed an eternity since he'd seen a familiar face and Parson's stunning appearance was as delightful as it was astonishing. Parsons looked thinner than when Smith had last seen him, but there was no mistaking his identity.

"Tell me what you're doing here," importuned Smith.

Parsons frowned and shook his head as if to clear it.

"I'm not completely sure. I was driving rather too fast and remember losing control of my car as I was negotiating a curve. I recall careening toward an embankment, and being terribly frightened, but nothing after that. I'm not even sure whether I collided with the embankment because the next thing I remember is walking along this road, which I have been doing for some time now, I think," he hazily responded. He looked around, quizzically. "Where *is* this place, Smith? And what are *you* doing here?" Parsons stared vaguely down the road, not really desiring a response because he already suspected the answers.

"Can we give you a ride somewhere?" Smith asked. Parsons appeared not to hear. "Can we give you a ride, Parsons?"

Parsons looked blankly at Smith and, after a long pause, responded, "No, thank you, Arthur. I think I'll just continue down this way for a while. Where are you going?"

"To Thule."

"Well, perhaps I'll see you again, Art. Yes?"

A bleak emptiness surge inside Smith before it dwindled into nihility, as when the illusion of redemption suddenly appears, only to shimmer quietly away.

"Yes, of course, but are you sure you won't join us?" Smith hollowly replied, though he could predict Parson's reply.

"No, I must see things for myself...you know, get established, in a manner of speaking." Parsons groped for words. "It's something that must be done by oneself. Like being born, I guess." He shrugged and vaguely smiled. Both men dried their tears.

"Goodbye, Art," Parsons said. He smiled again. "Be careful."

"Goodbye, Paul." Smith returned to his coach and slowly climbed in.

"That man is a friend?" Robin softly asked.

Smith nodded. "He was. And, if I cannot return home, perhaps I shall meet him again," he sighed.

Bread clucked his tongue and the cab lurched forward. Smith watched his friend resume shuffling down the road through the dust that boiled from beneath the wheels of the swaying coach.

"Arthur, look!" Robin blurted.

Smith turned from Parsons and followed her gaze. A large bird was silhouetted in the sky directly above them.

Smith watched his friend resume shuffling down the road through the dust that boiled from beneath the wheels of the swaying coach.

"It has been there since we departed the commander's office," she said. "And while you were talking to your friend, it perched in a tree until we again started moving. It is almost as though it is following us."

"It is," Smith angrily responded, immediately recognizing the Ansut. "We need to hurry," he urged Bread, who shook the reins, urging the horses to increase their gait.

Smith turned again to look rearward, but the coach had rounded a curve and Parsons' lonely form was completely lost from sight.

XXIII

Bread drove the coach directly to the home of Luman, a residence well-known due to the prominence of its occupant. It was with some trepidation that Smith stepped from the carriage upon their arrival in front of the modest structure. Though he searched the overhead sky as he assisted Robin to the ground, he saw no evidence of Lasceaux's feathered emissary

Requesting Bread and the escort to await them, Smith took Robin's arm and they ascended the few steps leading to the elevated porch of Luman's home. Knocking gently on the door, they heard the approach of footfalls from within. After a moment the door opened.

Framed within the doorway blinked a small, bespeckled old man with wispy white hair. He was dressed in a long robe and scuffed slippers.

"Are you Luman?" inquired Smith.

The old man smiled serenely. "I am. Who are you?"

"Two travelers seeking help. May we enter?"

"Certainly," said the old man without hesitation, motioning them in. Luman escorted them into a comfortable sitting room lined with bookcases whose shelves fairly sagged beneath the weight of the ponderous volumes occupying them. Directing them to chairs, Luman adjusted his robe and sat upon a hassock. "Now, my friends, what is the nature of the help you seek?"

Smith swallowed self-consciously. "I do not know exactly where to begin, sir."

"Begin where you will," smiled the aged man, "though it often proves fitting to begin at the beginning." A silence ensued as Smith considered the most efficacious manner in which to couch the reason for their unannounced visit. Robin nervously waited.

"Perhaps I can help," suggested Luman in due course. "You have come having lost something, hoping that I may be able to aid in its recovery. Am I correct?" Smith nodded. "That much is easily surmised," continued the augur, "but I daresay that yours is a rather remarkable case, judging from your mien. Again, I ask: what do you seek? Do not fear to speak openly, for I have seen and heard many improbable things in the course of my long life."

Impressed by Luman's perspicacity, Smith drew a deep breath. Robin reached across and squeezed his arm as he began speaking.

When he'd completed his narrative, Smith leaned back in his chair to observe Luman's reaction, whose snowy brow was pursed in thought.

"Of the alchemist, Lasceaux, I know much, most especially that he is a fool. But a dangerous fool," asserted the seer. "To have deceived him is rare, my children. To have deceived him and escaped death, unprecedented. But as you have learned, Lasceaux is an implacable foe. I do not fear him but you must, for it cannot be gainsaid that the alchemist is resolute and possesses malevolent skills."

"Yes, I know," said Smith, ruefully, as he recalled the alchemist's sulfurous Greek fire.

"Yet, it is a most curious thing," mused Luman, "that, in your exodus from the alchemist's lair, you did not chance into the elementals whose land you must certainly have traversed."

Smith was stunned, for out of consideration of their privacy he had made no mention of the gnomes, saying only that after escaping from Lasceaux, he had floated down the River Omer to Asem.

"You know of them?" he asked in astonishment.

"Indeed, though they know not of me!" laughed the old man. "You see, the River Omer is only a short distance from where we sit, and Asem only a day's journey. Smith was dumbfounded, for he was convinced that his adventures had taken him far afield.

"I apologize for my lack of absolute candor," he confessed. "The gnomes did provide me shelter, Luman. Is their existence generally known? They, themselves, are unaware of other peoples, save Lasceaux, his suppliers, and myself."

"On the contrary, I initially only suspected their existence, but surreptitious observation since that time has proven it. I may safely boast that few others have the slightest inkling of the elementals' existence. But that is as it should be."

Robin spoke for the first time. "I have encountered the alchemist but once, and I have never seen the elementals of whom you speak. But of one thing I am certain: Arthur does not belong in this world. He has been subject to ceaseless perils from the moment of his abduction. I, also, have suffered a smaller portion of the evils that have been his lot. You, Luman, are famed for your learning. Tell us plainly: can these things be set aright? Smith must be returned to his own world because he does not belong in ours. You and I *do* belong, but I am no longer happy here. Is it possible to leave this world and join him in his, thereby putting an end to these torments?" Robin's disconsolation was as expressive as her poignant entreaty. Smith was silent, for he could add nothing.

The wise old man listened carefully to Robin's plea. When she finished, he looked gravely at his guests.

"Alas, I am unable to provide a definitive response to your questions," he said, "for I have never undertaken what you propose. To pass between the synchronous planes of existence has been the desire of beings wise enough to comprehend their reality since time, itself, was young. Many have tried, many have failed. But a scant few in the history of the cosmos have effectuated such a passage and, of them, a fraction have returned to tell of it. Even in our time, a small number of savants have accomplished it. Their writings, for those who seek them out, inform us that certain sites constitute portals to parallel spheres, though few are aware of these gateways. Not far from here, in the woods bordering the River Omer, is such a site according to the esoteric texts. Near the crumbling ruin of an archaic castle is a pool of water, perpetually fed from beneath the surface of the ground. At the bottom of this pool reportedly lies the entrance to the coexistent world from whence Smith was taken, and to which you both desire to return. Whether or not such a return is possible I do not know for, although I am considered enlightened by some, I am in reality a mere philosophic embryo. Such modest gifts as I may possess flow entirely from the quills of those infinitely wiser than myself." He smiled and gestured toward the hundreds of books that lined the walls of the room. "I do not know whether they are *my* servants, or I am theirs."

"Do you consider it advisable to leave this place by means of that pool, if possible?" asked Smith.

"I consider it advisable to shun evil and embrace good," responded the old man, "and the beginning of good is harmony and order. To attain good, both properties must be present and in concord, for they are indispensable prerequisites. If they are absent or imbalanced it is essential to restore them."

As Smith mulled Luman's words, Robin spoke decisively.

"We must go," said she. "We have no alternative, for evil is even now snapping at our heels." She looked imploringly at Smith.

"Luman, how do we find this place you speak of?" he asked.

"Follow the road leading from Thule until you come to a lea. Leading from it you will see the vestiges of a path. Follow this path through the weald to a place of swamps, in the midst of which lay the ruins of the castle. Near them is the well rumored to be the threshold to other realms. Do not tarry...hasten there without delay, for the alchemist will not rest until he has exacted his vengeance."

Smith and Robin stood. "Thank you, Luman, for listening to us, and for your sympathy and help," said Smith. "I hope you enjoy all the blessings this world can provide."

The old man chuckled softly. "One is truly blessed who does not want. I wish you good luck and mourn that I am without power to further assist you. Whatever you do, children, loathe always evil and never cease to do good. All blessings proceed from these two principles. May the immortal gods preserve both of you."

XXIV

"Thank you for everything, Bread." So saying, Smith embraced the faithful sentry. "I'm afraid that Robin and I must carry on alone from here."

"But why? I beg you to allow us to accompany you to your destination to ensure your safety," insisted Bread.

"My enemy, Lasceaux, is powerful, and I fear that not even you can effectively combat him. The safety of all of us, at least for now, lies in flight until such time as the alchemist can finally be vanquished. My instinct is that his ultimate conqueror may be someone who possesses more strength than either of us." Even as Smith spoke, the wicked Ansut circled above them, squawking raucously.

"Arthur, we must hurry!" urged Robin as she looked fearfully about, anticipating the alchemist's imminent appearance.

"Goodbye, Bread." Smith again embraced him. "Please extend our thanks to Commander Tomkins, as well. Thank you for your kindnesses, my friend." Waving to the other guard, who still sat astride his mount, Smith grabbed Robin's hand and they hastened down the faint trail that led from the lea. A few moments later they paused and turned to look back. The Ansut still circled high overhead, but Bread and his companion had vanished.

Smith and Robin renewed their flight down the dim pathway.

***

After a short while, the land began to drop in elevation, becoming increasingly marshy. At its nadir the two sojourners finally came upon the remains of what was once, incalculably long ago, an imposing masonry edifice. Little more than crumbling piles of squared stones heaped upon the damp ground, the ruin still retained an air of magnificence and splendor, undiminished by the passage of countless ages. A solitary circular tower, more-or-less intact, loomed over the rubble.

Smith and Robin entered the tower through its empty doorway and carefully trod an interior curving staircase upward to its terminus. Beyond the parapet circumscribing the tower's summit they surveyed the surrounding woodland. Though they were unable to identify the mysterious pool spoken of by Luman, in the distance beyond the treetops they were able to distinguish the glint of sunlight upon a body of water.

"That must be the Omer," Smith speculated. "These ruins can't be too far from the Nustazien Highlands and the gnomes." The assurance of his friends' proximity partially assuaged Smith's anxieties, though Robin's fear remained unabated.

"Let us quickly find the pool which will take us from here," she admonished, peering nervously about. Eventide was not far off and the ambient light was already beginning to dim. Then she hissed, "Arthur, listen! Where is the Ansut?"

Smith listened attentively, but all he heard were frogs musically piping in the swamps that ringed the tower.

"Where is he?" he muttered, his voice on edge. Suddenly, inexplicably, even the sound of the frogs abruptly ceased.

"He is with me!" screamed a triumphant voice from across the marsh.

"Lasceaux!" Robin and Smith simultaneously blurted, though they were unable to identify the alchemist's exact location among the encircling trees.

"Lasceaux, indeed!" cried the alchemist. "The chase is over! Welcome home!" He howled madly, intoxicated with his achievement. "Nor do I come alone, for I am accompanied by legions!" Smith strained his eyes in the direction of the voice and, after a moment, spotted the pale form of the alchemist standing at the edge of the bog. The Ansut fluttered and squawked excitedly at the alchemist's feet. "The pool you seek is nearby, though you'll not make use of it...my minions shall see to that!"

From the surrounding forest emerged the alchemist's motley host, gathered from every pestilential cloaca and wretched murderers' den in the region. They completely encircled the ruins, precluding any possibility of escape.

"Rest well tonight, for the morrow shall see both of you dead," crooned the alchemist. With that, he gestured to his army, which drifted into the woods to gather fuel for cooking fires. Shortly thereafter, the besiegers settled around pleasant blazes. Lasceaux was prominent among the company and, in the fading sunlight, Smith also recognized a few seamen from the Harpy, notably associates of Rashid.

Atop the ruin, Smith and Robin grimly discussed their plight. Both felt reasonably confident the alchemist would not hazard a nocturnal assault, if only because he had no need to. Because it appeared impossible for them to slip through his lines, Lasceaux enjoyed the luxury of waiting until the following morning before storming the tower. As a consequence, they possessed a few hours of temporary security.

"I submit that we have two choices...we must try either to flee or, failing that, to fight. I fear we will fare poorly against the horde that currently menaces us, irrespective of our decision," Robin bravely stated. "If the former, we have very little time to attempt an escape."

They cautiously descended the stairs to the ground floor, where Smith began to grope his way along the unlit interior of their crumbling haven.

"Let's see how well this can be defended," he said over his shoulder.

Robin joined him as they undertook to investigate the enclosure. They rapidly determined that the circular chamber was relatively small with a smooth, paved floor. Its walls were devoid of any openings to the outside, save its collapsing doorway. Smith found this peculiar, since he had observed windows partway up the tower when they initially approached it earlier in the day. He quickly resumed groping along its curving interior wall. In short order his exploring fingers encountered the object he sought.

At eye-level, a hollow six inches deep was carved into the tower's stonework. Smith slid his hand upward about a foot and discovered another concavity; above it, yet another. They had until now taken no notice of the depressions.

"Robin!" he hissed.

In a moment she was at his side.

"Feel." He took her hand and guided it to the indentations.

"What are they?" she whispered.

"I think they're handholds chiseled into the masonry."

"Handholds? Where do they lead?"

"I don't know. There must be another story immediately above us that's bypassed by the staircase and accessed by these handholds...like a mezzanine. I'm going to try to climb up."

"I do not know what you mean by 'mezzanine,' but perhaps it is a hiding place."

Grasping the indentations with only his fingertips, and using his toes to dig into the crumbling stonework, Smith began a laborious ascent. Provided the strength in his fingers didn't fail him, he would be able to place his feet in the indentations after pulling himself upward far enough.

"Be careful, Arthur...you can't see where you are going," she importuned. It was by now pitch black inside the ruin.

"I will. Stand clear in case I fall," he panted.

He climbed with painful slowness and every few seconds Robin whispered, "Be careful!" from the darkness below.

"Yes, yes," he wheezed as he tortuously ascended. Once he was able to use his legs to full effect Smith was able to clamber upward with comparative rapidity and, at last, his head bumped against a wooden ceiling. He braced himself against the curved wall with one hand and reached overhead with the other. Using his fingertips, he traced the outline of a trapdoor.

"Hang on, I think I've found something," he told Robin, who waited anxiously below.

"Please be careful."

Smith could not help but smile as he balanced himself by placing both feet deep into the carved depressions while leaning into the concave stone wall. He slowly placed both of his palms flat against the wooden panel, paused to collect himself, then shoved as forcibly as he dared.

It didn't budge.

Smith readjusted his tottering position and strained his body further upward. He found that, by craning his neck sideways, he was able to awkwardly place one shoulder against the trapdoor. Pausing to re-establish firm footing, Smith then lunged upward in an attempt to dislodge the stubborn panel. As he did so, bits of mortar wedged around it cascaded downward. Smith gritted his teeth and, after another shove, the portal begrudgingly began to yield. Heartened, Smith pushed with even greater fervor as debris tumbled downward.

Alarmed by the falling detritus and the sounds of Smith's labor, Robin restlessly called, "Are you all right?"

"Yes. I think I dislodged the door to the second story." Smith used his hands to shove aside the heavy panel.

With effort, he managed to pull himself through the aperture into a round chamber where he collapsed, gasping and shaking from exertion.

To the extent Smith was able to determine in the darkness, the nondescript room appeared identical to the one below, except its stone walls were punctuated with window openings. Numerous chunks of stone and masonry littered its floor, apparently dislodged from its upper reaches sometime in the past.

"I'm here!" he finally called down to Robin.

"What did you find?"

"Just another room, but I can see better because it has windows. Hang on."

"Be careful," pleaded Robin.

Smith stood and picked his way across the room, where he warily peered out one of the windows.

Immediately beyond the marsh that encompassed the ruined tower, Smith could see Lasceaux's bivouac. A rapid glance through the remaining windows confirmed that the mob completely surrounded the ruin.

But an idea was already crystalizing in Smith's mind.

He descended the rudimentary ladder with far more confidence that he had ascended it and drew Robin near. In hushed tones, he disclosed to her his plan.

Robin did not interrupt while Smith spoke but, when he'd concluded, said, "Your idea holds promise but is too obvious for the two of us to attempt.

Furthermore, for you to undertake it alone would be foolish because Lasceaux will be certain to recognize you. Lasceaux does not know *me*, however. Alone, I might succeed in getting through and summoning aid."

"No, Robin. I won't hear of it," protested Smith.

"Think, Arthur, *think!*" she urgently countered. We are sure to get caught if we attempt your stratagem together. And even you, by yourself, will fail! But I am a virtual stranger to Lasceaux because he saw me only once, and that briefly, in Commander Tomkin's quarters. I, alone, might succeed."

"It's too dangerous!"

Robin clutched his hand. "The morrow will witness our deaths, Arthur. *Think*! My way is our only hope!"

Smith sat silently for many minutes. Then he said very, very softly, "I fear you are right. Do you want to try?"

A broad smile of relief illuminated Robin's face in the darkness. She hugged Smith for a long time, "Yes," she said.

XXV

Smith returned to the tower from the edge of the marsh, from whose shallows he gathered bunches of milk-thistle and wild cranberry. None of the alchemist's inebriated troops had observed his foray. Now inside once again, he sat near the open doorway next to Robin, where the army's camp fires provided a half-light. By their flickering illumination he squeezed sticky white sap from the milk-thistles and smeared it on Robin's face, hands, and arms. Before it thoroughly dried, he crushed the cranberries and patted the crimson bits onto her skin. Robin took dirt from the floor and began rubbing it into her hair and clothing.

Smith forced a smile as he worked, but was plagued by doubt. He paused and took Robin's hands in his. "I'm having second thoughts...I'm not sure this will work."

She nodded gravely. "You are right, Arthur. It probably will not succeed. But if it does not, we will be no worse off than before. If we do nothing, we will simply pass our time until tomorrow morning, when we will be murdered by Lasceaux. Alternatively, if we make an effort to escape while we still can, though those efforts are not ultimately crowned with success, we will be murdered tonight, instead. Our prospects are bleak, either way."

Smith nodded. "It's about as long as it is broad, I suppose. But it's not too late for us to change places. Even if Lasceaux captures me tonight, he may agree to spare you."

"He will not spare me, Arthur," she sighed. "The alchemist will award me to his companions and, when they finally grow bored with me, they will simply kill me."

In his heart, Smith knew that Robin's reasoning was unassailable. He said nothing further but devoted himself to enhancing her masquerade.

***

Their combined labors ultimately produced a disguise that met with their mutual satisfaction.

Robin stood and whirled in place. "Do I look adequately loathsome?"

Smith climbed to his feet. "Perfectly hideous."

"Thank you, Arthur," she curtsied. "Shall we proceed? If we wait until we are ready, we shall never be ready."

"In a moment." Smith stepped close to Robin and wordlessly pulled her to him. They embraced in silence.

"I must go now," she finally whispered. "All will be well, Arthur."

Smith released her and stepped to the open doorway.

***

"Robin! There's somebody in here!" he shouted at the top of his voice. He hoped the encircling army heard his exclamation. "God spare us...it's a *leper*!"

"Leave us!" screamed Robin. "Oh, God, what a monster! Arthur, *do* something!"

Smith peered toward the alchemist's encampment. Across the bog he could see a number of figures silhouetted against their fading campfires, presumably listening.

"Leave us! Leave us, horrid thing!" Robin shrieked.

Smith embraced her again. "Good luck, Robin," he whispered. "I pray for your escape."

"I will return, Arthur. You may rely on it. Do not despair." The eyes of both brimmed with tears. "Await me." With that, she stepped to the doorway.

Hearing the commotion, the alchemist ordered his minions to ascertain its cause. What they immediately observed was a disheveled figure hurtle from the ruin and tumble to the ground.

"You blackguards cannot do this to me!" screamed the figure toward the tower. "I am but a defenseless old woman whose only sanctuary lies in this ruin. It is an affront to the universe that two rogues can simply burst into my home without hindrance and cast me out! May whatever cruel gods rule over us despise and curse you for your shameful cowardice!"

Lasceaux's forces burst into laughter upon witnessing this histrionic display, their imaginations providing for them what their senses could not. In their mind's-eye they pictured their two captives blundering into a pathetic, diseased old woman who had taken shelter in the tower, and summarily expelling her from her adopted home.

Hearing their laughter, Robin spun toward them. "And who are you brutes?" she derisively yelled. "Confederates of the scoundrels who cast me from my own hearth?"

"Nay, grandmother," mocked one of them, "we are agents of the gods, sent to avenge you!" His taunting retort caused his comrades to guffaw.

"Then praise be to them," said Robin. She struggled to her feet and began threading her way through the fingers of the marsh toward her ostensible saviors. "The gods act swiftly," she marveled aloud, inciting additional laughter at her credulity.

Half-way across the bog, she turned and shook her fist at the ruin. "You two will suffer for your banditry!" She shook her fist yet again. From inside the ruin, Smith watched her passage in silent anguish.

Robin continued hobbling slowly toward the rabble, but as she drew nigh to their guttering fires one of the men gasped, "By the gods, she is a leper! No wonder they cast her out."

"A leper!" murmured several horrified watchers, and the appalling news began to race through the entire company. "Come no further!" warned those within its ranks.

The skeptical Lasceaux stepped to the forefront. "Nay, approach closer," he wheedled. "Let us see you clearly." Several around him groused their disapproval, but a baleful look from the alchemist immediately silenced them.

Robin swallowed nervously and began advancing toward Lasceaux as his followers shrank from her. Smith anxiously watched her performance from the doorway of the wrecked tower though, because of the distance, was unable to discern the alchemist's words.

"Halt!" commanded the alchemist when Robin drew within ten feet of him. The yellowish light of a dying campfire flickered irregularly on her downturned face. Lasceaux peered at her unsightly countenance in the uncertain illumination it provided. "You resided in the ruin?"

Robin mutely nodded.

"Look at me!" he screeched. Robin slowly raised her head and nodded again. "Why, then, do you pollute us with your odious presence?"

"Those criminals are to blame for my misfortunes." Robin spoke in a guttural tone to camouflage her voice.

"Who?"

"Those monsters...a man and his wench. They cast me out but I have nowhere to go. No one will harbor me."

"How many remain in the tower?"

"A rogue and his wench, as I stated," she responded. "I implore the gods to strike them down with the same pestilence that ravages me."

The alchemist gazed toward the dark ruin and smirked. "You are only partly correct, lazar. While doubtless no one would be mad enough to harbor you in your contemptible condition, it is *you* who are truly the monster. Unless you wish to forfeit the few blighted days remaining to you, make your way from this place without delay, else you contaminate the very air by your detestable nearness." He stepped aside, clearing the way for Robin to pass.

"But where shall I go? Where shall I go?" she muttered as she stumbled forward, though she was already certain of her destination. Smith had instructed her to make her way toward the Omer then head upriver. The gnomes were certain to accost Robin once she entered their territory...hopefully, that would be sooner, rather than later...whereupon she could apprise them of Smith's desperate plight and solicit their aid. Until then, Smith would attempt to defend his position against the alchemist's coming assault.

He watched Robin merge with the night beyond the alchemist's bivouac with mixed feelings of gladness and despair.

XXVI

Following Robin's exodus, Smith again ascended to the second story of the tower, whose windowed heights, he decided, afforded a superior defensive position. He weighted down the trapdoor with heavy pieces of block and molding then set himself to monitoring the movement of the hostile army encamped virtually at his feet.

***

Except for the sentries that hemmed the ruins, Lasceaux's army slept until well past dawn. The sun was already high when he finally marshalled his forces and crossed the bog to stand at the very base of the tower, three men deep.

"They are in the throes of terror arising from the certainty of imminent death, an agony vastly crueler than that of even death, itself," the alchemist lectured hirelings eager to commence the offensive. "I derive exquisite pleasure from the horror that grips them and have no desire, through the expedient of quick deaths, to provide succor from their crippling dread."

Because of the constricted aperture leading to the interior of the tower, the attackers would necessarily be compressed tightly together upon storming it, thus hampering their assault and providing an easy target for the stone missiles that Smith had assembled near him. Armed only with rudimentary weapons, Lasceaux's motley army relied on sheer force of numbers to overrun Smith's tenuous defenses.

The alchemist ordered one of his men to creep forward and reconnoiter the interior of the tower. Begrudgingly compliant, the man fearfully approached the doorway and stuck his head inside while his fellows braced themselves, lest an unexpected blow from within deprive him of his pate. From his perch above, Smith could see that the man was visibly relieved to find the ground floor room unoccupied.

"So our little birds have abandoned their nest," crooned Lasceaux upon hearing his report. "They could not have flown without our knowledge, however." He stepped back a few paces and faced the second story windows. "Smith!" he cried, "surrender yourself now and I will spare the maiden. Resist and both of you will perish!"

Smith promptly replied by heaving a chunk of mortar at him, which missed badly.

"So be it!" screeched the alchemist. "Seize them both!"

The mob nearest the door began shoving and shouldering its way into the tower. Smith responded with a bombardment of lithic projectiles. In their frantic haste to evade them, the besiegers frenetically pushed forward with even greater intensity, creating a near total blockage of the doorway. Though most of the rocks landed on the shoulders of Smith's attackers, some cracked unprotected heads. Despite this, his targets were unable to elude the hailstorm because of the developing pandemonium.

At the rear of the grunting mass, Lasceaux, shouted orders to his beleaguered army.

"Retreat, you fools! Retreat!" he screamed. In frustration, the alchemist rushed to the rearmost attacker, grabbed him, and flung him to the ground. Without pausing, he did the same to another, then another, then another, until the entire line capitulated in disorganized retreat.

Smith hurled chunks of stone at the fleeing mob until it was out of effective range. Beneath him on the ground lay the bodies of a half-dozen of the alchemist's minions, either crushed and trampled by their own comrades or the victims of Smith's rocky barrage. Partly out of nervousness, partly out of relief, Smith laughed uproariously at the sight.

"Come and get us!" he jeered, nearly delirious in the exuberance that is often born of fear.

"Go and collect dry wood," Lasceaux commanded, undeterred. "We shall soon see how merrily they mock the flames."

In short order a pile of what little burnable wood remained in the area after the previous night's campfires lay before the alchemist. Smith, meanwhile, used the respite to replenish his stock of ammunition.

"Now, go and collect some of those stones," continued the alchemist. "We shall pay them back in the same coin." Braving the missiles that Smith aimed at them, two hardy individuals raced back to the tower and began gathering the rocks that lay strewn about the ground. Quickly realizing their objective, however, Smith ceased providing them further munitions.

"By twos, fill your arms with wood, carry it into the ruin, and deposit it onto the floor," Lasceaux instructed. "When a sufficient amount has been collected, we shall burn them out."

Two men gathered armloads of wood and trotted toward the tower doorway, while others lobbed well-aimed volleys of stones through the window to keep Smith at bay. When the first pair of carriers returned, two more set out with additional fuel.

Lasceaux clapped his hands in delight and, from the boughs of a nearby tree, the Ansut glided down to him.

"Go and see how our little birds prepare for the conflagration," he ordered. The bird flapped clumsily toward the tower's second story, where it perched on a window ledge and scrutinized the interior. Although Smith heaved a rock at the spy, the Ansut easily avoided it and departed.

"In what manner to they prepare for their deaths?" Lasceaux gloated, rubbing his bony hands together, after the bird returned.

"'They'? Master, there is but one inside."

A horrified expression clouded the alchemist's visage. "What?"

"There is but one inside the tower...the wench is gone."

"That is impossible. Where could she be?" Lasceaux babbled.

"Here, Lasceaux!"

The alchemist turned and beheld Robin stepping from the tree line.

"Capture her!" he barked.

Before anyone could comply, however, the woods exploded in a myriad of elementals. From his vantage, Smith could see the gnomes swarm from all sides. In an instant, they fell upon Lasceaux's bewildered army, sweeping through their ranks without hesitation, overwhelming all resistance. The Ansut, itself, was among the first to perish: caught completely by surprise and unable to spread its large wings in time to gain the safety of the trees, one of the gnomes was upon it in the twinkling of an eye. The dryad grabbed the beast and dispassionately snapped its thin neck.

Mercenary after mercenary fell beneath the violent storm, their bodies broken with ruthless efficiency by the elementals. In the midst of the debacle, Robin endeavored to pick her way toward the tower.

"Arthur! Arthur!" she anxiously called.

But the alchemist, who also sought the ruin in order to escape the tempest that had descended upon him, heard her.

"Faugh!" he roared. "This is *your* doing!" He leapt at Robin but her attempt to elude his grasp was in vain.

In a single bound, Lasceaux reached her and snatched her delicate throat in his scaly hands. She fought against him violently, but for naught; the alchemist crushed her neck like a bandbox. When she fell limp in his hands, he hurled Robin's lifeless body to the ground and raced through the milling throng to the tower, from whose height Smith had witnessed the entire wretched act in stunned disbelief.

"Lasceaux!" he screamed. Smith darted across the room and kicked away the debris that covered the trap door. Flinging it open, he started to descend to the chamber below when the alchemist stormed into the tower.

"Lasceaux!" Smith again cried. The alchemist's eyes glittered with rage when he looked upward at Smith.

"You will now join your wench in the sleep from which there is no awakening," he hissed. Outside the thick walls of the tower the rout of the alchemist's ragtag army was nearly complete, though neither paid it any heed.

"You hide like a fearful rabbit," Lasceaux snarled. He began pulling himself upward on the stone ladder.

Smith backed away from the trap door and prepared to lash out with a kick to the alchemist's head the instant it appeared through the portal. Anticipating such an attack, Lasceaux sprang into the room with astonishing agility, causing the blow to sail wide.

"You cretin," he grinned, exposing broken stumps of teeth. "Your strumpet is dead and your own miserable existence nears its end."

The alchemist slowly circled Smith as he slipped a hand into his filthy robe. When he withdrew it, he held something.

"Recall this?" he sneered as he tossed its contents at his adversary.

Smith leapt aside as the infernal Greek fire fell harmlessly to the floor. The alchemist withdrew yet another handful and cast it at Smith, who jumped safely away.

"Yes, jump, jump!" Lasceaux gleefully gibbered as he continued to circle. "Jump, little rabbit!"

Smith stumbled over a chunk of masonry on the floor but managed to retain his balance. Without taking his eyes off the stalking alchemist, he stooped to pick it up.

As Lasceaux reached for more of his blistering powder, Smith responded through clenched teeth, "No, I don't think I will. *You* jump," and heaved the stone at the alchemist with all his strength.

Because of the swiftness of his attack, the stout trajectile caught Lasccaux squarely on the forehead but, miraculously, did not knock him to the floor. Despite this, Smith could see a look of utter shock register on the countenance of the alchemist, only to disappear behind a curtain of yellow fluid bubbling from the wound above his eyes.

Lasceaux wobbled on his feet, clutching his face in his hands.

"You fool!" he cursed. "Your treachery has just assured you a more painful death."

The alchemist stumbled toward Smith and blindly extended his clawed hands. Benefiting from Lasceaux's helplessness, Smith bounded toward him and seized the front of his rotting cloak. The alchemist frantically pawed at his eyes in an effort to clear them of the glistening secretion as he attempted to struggle free of Smith's grip.

Smith doubled up his fist and, drawing it back, launched it at the enraged alchemist's face.

The blow snapped Lasceaux's head back and propelled him backward on his heels. His momentum as he recoiled from the blow was so great that he careened across the rock-strewn floor, toward the open trap door. Too late the alchemist looked down with blurred vision to glimpse for an instant the yawning portal.

Then his body vanished without a sound.

Quivering from the adrenalin coursing through his body, Smith stepped to the trapdoor and looked down, to the lower chamber.

Lasceaux's broken form lay in death upon the pile of wood that was intended as Robin's and Smith's pyre.

XXVII

"Our hearts grieve as one for thy loss," King Gob said. "Be it any solace to thee, our ancestors counsel us that, though this house of clay may perish, our vital essence abides in perpetuity. The whole of our existence is indelibly engraved upon the cosmos and requires only the proper spark to blossom into remembrance. Perhaps Robin and ye may one day be reunited in another place, if it be so deigned; those who seek with a pure heart are seldom disappointed. Until then, 'In perpetuam rei memoriam' it is said in the venerable tongue: nothing is so lasting as our memories. Thine for Robin, but also hers, wherever she now exists, for thou."

The elementals had prepared Robin's remains for conveyance to their ancient catacombs, where they would be accorded a tomb of especial sanctity within its venerable halls. The bodies of Lasceaux and his minions were haphazardly gathered into a tumulus preparatory to burning, while the surviving remnants of the alchemist's motely army had previously abandoned the field in disordered panic.

"Return to thy world, Smith. Although thou possess boundless cause to weep stinging tears, depart with the thought that one day ye and Robin may well meet again, and on that day no amount of adversity shall separate thee."

"Holla! Here it is!" Bolander's voice carried over the swampy ground from beyond a copse of trees.

"Come." Gob gently grasped Smith's arm and assisted him to his feet. They walked the 50 yards to where Bolander, Milo, and several others stood by a small freshwater pond.

Smith paused at its edge and gazed across its surface, rippled slightly by the gentle inflow of subterranean water.

"We have searched the area thoroughly, and this pond is the only such body in the vicinity," affirmed Bolander. "I daresay that it is the one thou seeketh."

Gob looked up at Smith. "How did Luman instruct thee to return?"

"He said the portal to my world lies at the bottom," Smith replied, completely without spirit.

"Then find it and return thither. Do not squander further time here...all things have a natural place. Know that whatever vicissitudes befall thee anon, thou shalt always have friends here." Gob reached into his pocket and withdrew an enormous diamond. "Beware of thieves," he cautioned with a twinkle in his eye.

Smith took the gem, reached down and lifted the stout little man.

"Goodbye, Gob." He hugged him then did the same for Milo and Bolander. "Goodbye, my friends!" he cried, and his voice cracked as he addressed the rest of the party who had assembled around the pond. "God bless you all."

"We have been abundantly blessed," Gob assured him.

"Goodbye!" cried Smith again. He turned, looked down into the clear water, took a deep breath, and dove in.

The pond was warm and clear. Smith swam rapidly toward the bottom and, once there, looked about as best he could for a door of some kind. But the pond was deep and the light filtering through the water dim.

Smith searched quickly but could find no portal of any sort. Becoming lightheaded from holding his breath, he planted his feet on the muddy bottom and launched himself toward the surface, chagrinned and disappointed.

He shot through the surface of the pond and expelled the pent-up air in his lungs with a great gasp.

***

Smith treaded water and blinked his eyes to dispel the droplets that clouded his vision. Around the perimeter of the pond, where moments before stood the elementals, were spindly trees and cacti. He looked around in confusion.

Smith swam to the edge and climbed out. A brilliant late afternoon sun beat down on him. Slowly, very slowly, the reality of his circumstances began to coalesce in his disoriented mind.

Around the perimeter of the pond, where moments before stood the elementals, were spindly trees and cacti.

Smith stepped beyond the growth that encircled the pond. Three hundred yards away, on the apex of a low hill, rose the solitary remains of an old smoke stack. Below them, in a valley less than a half-mile distant, lay a scattering of buildings.

Smith was home, though exactly *where* he knew not.

Wearily, he began plodding toward the settlement and, as the shadows began to lengthen, encountered a dirt road and a battered sign:

MAYER, ARIZONA
ELEV. 4500 FEET

Smith sighed and continued down the road. He still remembered Freeman's telephone number and hoped he could induce someone in Mayer to lend him a cell phone.

— The End —

Also available from

WF Waldrip

⭐⭐⭐⭐⭐ **great novel!**

What a wonderful novel! The author drew very vivid pictures of the characters and events. What a riveting book! A fascinating read !

Published on June 3, 2014 by Vincent R. Mayr

Find more at www.amazon.com

Also available from

WF Waldrip

Honor Among
Thieves

WF Waldrip

☆☆☆☆☆ **An Excellant Sequel**

By michael caburis on October 12, 2014

Format: Kindle Edition   Verified Purchase

A riviting sequel to The Guards Themselves .
i hope another by the author is forthcoming
WF Waldrip is a must read author

Find more at www.amazon.com

Also available from

WF Waldrip

⭐⭐⭐⭐⭐ **Steven King can relax**

By Doug T. on March 14, 2018

Format: Paperback   Verified Purchase

Steven King can rest easy and retire knowing Wade Waldrip can carry the torch and scare the wits out of people.

Find more at www.amazon.com

Also available from

WF Waldrip

⭐⭐⭐⭐⭐ **Lots of twists and surprises**
April 25, 2019
Format: Kindle Edition

A really fun book to read (wish it was a lot longer), you can't read the first 10 pages and guess the ending like so many books, the plot turns and surprises you, really enjoyed reading it. Also enjoyed the characters depth. I'm from Phoenix AZ and got a kick reading about the familiar places and businesses.

Find more at www.amazon.com

WF Waldrip

WF WALDRIP is a widely traveled author, and Arizona native.

His writing style is true to life, bypassing the 'Politically Correct."

www.ingramcontent.com/pod-product-compliance
Lightning Source LLC
Chambersburg PA
CBHW071853220626
47052CB00002B/106